Dr Keerth is a 1997-born doctor by profession and a writer by passion, originally hailing from a small town in Tamil Nadu, Tirunelveli, and currently working as a Medical Officer in Odisha. The two things that fascinate her the most are ancient civilisations and outer space. This is her first story, and with this, she is finally beginning the career of her dreams.

732 Miles
by Dr. Keerth
Paperback Edition

First Published in India in 2022
by Inkfeathers Publishing, New Delhi 110095

Copyright © Dr. Keerth 2022
Illustrations by Baskar
Map on the cover is sourced from
http://www.columbia.edu/itc/mealac/pritchett/00maplinks/
modern/maps1947/randmcnallynorthmax.jpg

ISBN 9789390882441

www.inkfeathers.com

732 MILES

How far would one go for survival?

DR.KEERTH

Inkfeathers Publishing
www.inkfeathers.com

உள்ளுவ தெல்லாம் உயர்வுள்ளல் மற்றது
தள்ளினுந் தள்ளாமை நீர்த்து.

Let thoughts always be great and grand
Though they fail their virtues stand.

—*Kural 596*

To where it all began,

My alma mater,

Pushpalata Vidya Mandir, Tirunelveli.

CONTENTS

ACKNOWLEDGEMENTS

Straight from my heart,

The world is a better place because of you all and it's important for me to let you know how much I value each and every one of you.

First of all, this book would have been impossible without Dr Vimal Adityan, my senior in college and my dearest friend. Even if I put the best of the words and get help from the best of the poets, it would still be insufficient to put in words how much you mean to me. You are my number-one supporter. Thank you for being there every single day, every single time, on every single chapter, and throughout my journey; and not just being there, but helping me with this book, day and night, like it was your own book. You were the first person to whom I narrated the story, and you were the one who encouraged me to make that story into a book. Thank you for everything, Vimal.

Appa and Amma (Dr Soundararaja and Dr Subbu Lakshmi) for giving me all the freedom to explore various fields and find my areas of interest. To them, I owe not only my genes, but also all that I have and all that I am now. Thank you.

My sincere gratitude to Dr Shreemathy for being the best senior one could ever ask for. The days I used to regret for not having an elder sibling are long gone. I have you now, and I love you with all my heart. Getting you in my life was the best thing that ever happened during our college days.

Thank you to my pal, Dr Lakshmi, for believing in me. I love you, Laksh. I would never get bored of writing about us. If I were to sum up our relationship in a line, 'You are like the Red while I am the Andy.' If at all there comes a day where I end up in Zihuatanejo alone, I would only leave a letter to you and take you with me. That's how much I love you.

I am indebted to my professors from college: Dr Ajit Kumar, Dr Karthik, and Dr Nirmal from the Dept. of Orthopaedics, for giving me the best days of CRRI. You made me feel home in college, and easily, you are the best professors that I got to work with. Thank you for everything.

My profound thanks to Dr Vijay Balaji from the Dept. of General Medicine (then) and now Gastroenterologist at CMC, Vellore—considering you as my professor or my mentor would be such an understatement. You are more like my dearest friend, my stardust, and the only reason behind my affinity towards Medicine postings.

Dr Aishwarya from the Dept. of Anaesthesia: Ma'am, thank you for being such a sweetheart. The days you are "on duty" are my favourite days of the week any time. Thank you for taking me under the warmth of your wings. I will always, always love you.

Then, my sincere thanks goes to Dr Anuj Srinivasan from the Dept. of Surgery. I would never forget your words. You had been the impetus for me to have a craving for story writing which began back in college days, when I was in my 2nd year. And you had been one among the Jury in a creative writing event. Not just giving the first place, you also took your time to encourage me in person about my writing and that made all the difference.

It's worth to mention Dr Pugazhenthi from the Dept. of Community Medicine. It is because of teachers like you that students like me grow.

I cannot thank Dr Rock Britto (Dept. of Community Medicine), Dr Rashid Khan (Dept. of Biochemistry), Dr Jesudoss (Dept. of ENT), Dr Gurudatta Pawar (Dept. of Forensic Medicine), and Dr Karthik (Dept. of Surgery) enough for being the best teachers one could ever ask for. I have immense respect on all of you.

My heartfelt thanks to my seniors in college—Dr Arunagiri, Dr Sriram, Dr Nevetha, Dr Greeshma, Dr Rishi, and Dr Marzuk for being the best seniors and making my college days less painful. Similarly, my hearty thanks to my juniors in the college—Dr Soniya, Dr Ashly, Dr Sunil, Dr Ram, Dr Swetha, and Dr Bhuvanesh for being my all-time cheerleaders.

My batch mates and my favourite companions, Dr Jothimai and Dr Indhu Malini, I would like to express that I have been extremely comfortable when you guys are around. And I loved spending every day of CRRI with you.

Thanks to my roommates Dr Hemalatha and Dr Nivedhita for putting up with me all those years.

And, Dr Madhumita, I would undoubtedly say, if selflessness was a person, then it would have your image. Mere thanking you will not suffice all that you had done to me. You have stood behind me during the most important times and also when nobody else did. I will remember you as long as I live and be grateful to you as long as I breathe.

Saravanan, Siva, Indiran, Ram Krishnan, and Mukilan from my family for giving me their time and I can't thank you enough for encouraging me to choose the road not taken.

Ashania, Aafila, and Afrah Shabnam, from being my girls at school to being my bridesmaids, you three have my heart. I was fortunate enough to have attended high school with these amazing people.

Sujitha, Raaji, Jenifer, Rijo, Sankar, and Mohideen Haji—I am intensely gifted and blessed to get such fabulous friends at school. I am so glad that I had you growing up.

Joseph Sir, from Rosemary School, I thank you wholeheartedly for believing in me. They say, 'There is no bad student, only a bad teacher.' I would rather put it this way, 'There is no great student, only great teachers,' Even if the entire school hated me, you would always be there to encourage me in your own subtle way. I wish every student gets a teacher like you.

Thanks to Hanah Moin, Shanmuga Priya, Farzana, Sripal Bhansali, and Selva Sundari for being the most supportive and wonderful friends in PVM. I had my best years of school life with you guys.

My devoted thanks to my English Professor, Ms Sheila Sharon, then Vice Principal at Pushpalata Vidya Mandir. I'm here today because of you, ma'am.

My sincere thanks goes to a few other teachers from school, Bindhu ma'am, Jhansi ma'am, Ramji Sir, and Rajalakshmi ma'am for pushing me to aim for the stars.

I can never miss thanking Mohideen Abdul Kader. In spite of being continents apart, you have always had a greater part in all my benchmarks and I'm sure you are going to be there with me with all my endeavours in the upcoming days.

I equally thank Zahir Sir, my mentor for life and my physics teacher since Class 9. I have completed 12 years of schooling and 5 and a half years of college studies, and even now if somebody asks me, 'Who is the best teacher in the world?' I would just close my eyes and name you. That's the impact you made on me. Undoubtedly, you are the best teacher. I would honestly suggest people who dread physics, just attend his class at least once.

My thanks to Vetri, Shivram, and Devi. You all have played small yet significant roles in my life. I strongly believe that my thank-you page would be incomplete without mentioning you all. I will remember the three of you forever.

I thank Neeraj Rao Sir, from Vision IAS, for explaining historical information in a fascinating way. This story is a direct outcome of listening to all your ancient and modern history lectures. Nobody can make histories more interesting than you.

My heartfelt thanks to the YouTube channel "Indian Military History" for giving me insights on the battle sequences and my publishing team of Inkfeathers for making my dream come true.

Also, I would thank Director Vetrimaaran from the bottom of my heart. The whole time, I have always visualised how 732 Miles would have been, if you had directed it. Big fan of your work, Sir.

My partner, Dr Kali, the day you came into my life, it completely changed and changed for the good. Dr Keerth came into existence because of you. You are the best and my most favourite critic. I love how incredibly intelligent you are and how you have been shaping me slowly into this much better version of me.

And finally, but most importantly, thank you Guhan for being my rock, my brother, and my best friend. Not just this book, your name is going to be there in all my future books to come. Thank you for being a remarkable support to me. There is a saying, 'Some people make you feel safe in this world,' but you have made me fearless. If I ever get to demand a "trial by combat" in real life, I would name you as my champion without any doubt. (That's how much I trust you with my life and I am pretty sure you would win anything if it was for me). My book and my life are better because I have you.

PROLOGUE

January 25, 2021
New Delhi, India

It is a placid afternoon, silent like the calm after the storm. A few women are packing up all the things inside the house and arranging them in brown carton boxes. Boxes are first sealed and then labelled. Almost half of the house is empty. Relatives and friends, who came last week, all have left. The house and everything around it stands still, just like her life. Not even a leaf moves that day.

There is a squeaking sound of a not-so well-maintained wheelchair inside the house. She is in her 70's, wearing a floral white dress and a lavender sweater. She is old and pale. Her grey strands shine like silver, loosely made into a low bun. Years of history are buried deep in her memory, her eyes reflecting a peculiar opacity, a testament of all the years that had passed. Every wrinkle on her face shouts the story of her survival. Her veins are visible as green threads along her forearms as she struggles to make the chair move and navigate herself to the hall. She cannot move without the help of her wheelchair these days.

She stops in front of the white wall in the main room and stares at a picture of a man framed and hung on the wall. He is in his 40's, with deep brown eyes and well-groomed hair. A string of flowers hangs around his frame. It's been 2 weeks since he has passed away. It is her son, Amir.

She keeps thinking of the number of houses that she had to shift since she was born. After all these years, none of them felt like her home. She had come to Delhi from Firozpur after her marriage. She lost her mother to cardiac arrest 30 years back, and her husband, Azaan, martyred in the Siachen conflict in 1985. He was a team member of the Operation Meghdoot. She had brought up her only son, Amir, alone all these years. He had been her last ray of hope in her long-lost country.

Her eyes are brimming with tears as she keeps wondering about everything that she had lost, and even her tears do not come down easily as if they are depleted from crying for the past 2 weeks.

She strolls through the main room, and gazes out of the window, contemplating the complexity of her life here in Delhi. At the corner, she finds some books stacked, ready to be packed.

She is shifting her house again. She is leaving Delhi and moving back to Rawalpindi, Pakistan, which is where she has decided to spend her last days. The day that she wished would never come has finally arrived. Tomorrow, she will leave India once and for all.

The stack of books near her collapses and falls one after another. She bends down and picks up the first book, dusts it, and her eyes go over the title. It was written by her brother. The hardcover reads 'The line that changed my life' by Abhimanyu Dayanand. She had read that book a few times before. But today, she feels like reading it once again. After all, it was the line that had changed her life, too.

Abhimanyu was a celebrated writer in India back in the 1970s. He is no more now, but he was once the voice of hundreds of commons. He always took up true stories from people all over India and penned them down. His biggest bestseller and his most famous story was this—his own story. The story that shaped his life and millions of others. It's the story of the line that fell right through the hearts of people, piercing them too deep to leave a scar for a lifetime.

She slowly opens the book and finds blurry lines moving all over and calls for Jothi for her spectacles. Jothi, her help, has been taking care of her for the past few years. There is nothing she can do on her own these days. She gets the spectacles from Jothi, wears them, takes a deep breath, and finally begins to read Chapter 1…

Chapter One

BIRTHDAY

August 14, 1947

10:52 p.m.

Rawalpindi, Pakistan

With people thronging the streets, soaring with nationalism, the spirit of newfound freedom booming, Pakistan was celebrating its birthday. Among all this chaos was Bhavna wailing and screaming so loud that the walls enclosing her would shatter any minute. She was in labour; it was her first baby. Her water had broken earlier that day and the baby's head was about to get crowned. As the intensity of her uterine contractions increased, so did her agony. She was panicking.

Devi Ma, the eldest midwife in Rawalpindi, had been Bhavna's caretaker since her mother passed away when she was six. Devi Ma had conducted innumerable deliveries. Quite literally, every other child that was born in her neighbourhood in the last 20 years had been pulled out by her. But this was different. It was Bhavna (Bhavi).

'You want a boy or a baby girl, Bhavi?' Devi Ma asked. 'A girl baby… for sure,' she replied with a smile.

'Only pain can bring the baby out, just bear it for some time; you are surely going to get a baby girl.' Devi Ma comforted her as she applied a towel squeezed in hot water on her pelvis.

The warmth helped her with the pain but not for long.

As the baby's head descended further down, it hurt like hell. As any spouse would have wanted, Bhavna yearned for Kabir's presence. She screamed as if her body was being torn apart; there was Kabir, waiting outside the house, contemplating all the scary things that might happen in the days to come. Though he was outside the delivery room, every bit of him wished to be with Bhavi. He loved her. He loved her so dearly. But they wouldn't allow him inside, and all he could do was just pray for fortitude.

Her labour pains were starting to take another form. She was dripping in sweat, her face had gone pale, and she went on screaming, but she never gave up. She had an indomitable spirit. Even if one had been concretely preparing this for a lifetime, it wouldn't still be adequate. Can you imagine pushing another miniature human out of your body?

Flashback

*Kabir was born to **Mohideen Abdul Kader**, a freedom fighter, and an ardent follower of Bhagat Singh, from Firozpur, Punjab. Mohideen was a man of honour who brought up Kabir as a single parent. During World War II, Mohideen was a soldier in the British-Indian Army, fighting Japan. Along with the other prisoners of war, he joined the Azad Hind Army under the leadership of Subhash Chandra Bose whilst leading the Jawaharlal Nehru regiment.*

WW-II

It was the biggest conflict in history that had lasted almost six years (1939-1945), between the Axis Powers (Italy, Germany, and Japan) and the Allies (France, Great Britain, The United States, and The Soviet Union). India was reluctant in the participation of war as it was not directly Indian war, but British. India's participation was by accident as she was the colony of Britain at that time. India contributed more than 2 million soldiers, thousands of cattle, and millions of tonnes of food grains as the food supply for the allied soldiers, and because of that, India had to sacrifice thousands of her citizens and had to suffer wartime miseries. In the Bengal famine of 1943, around 3 million Bengalis perished of hunger which occurred due to the diversion of food grains from Bengal to the allied army.

Azad Hind Army

During the outbreak of World War II, Japan invaded Southeast Asia. More than 50000 Indians, belonging to the British-Indian Army, were stationed in the Malayan and Singapore region. Britain lost Singapore to Japan, and in the Singapore campaign alone, 45000 Indian prisoners of war were captured. It was from those prisoners our first INA (Indian National Army) was formed under the leadership of Mohan Singh, a former officer from the British-Indian Army. The initiative received a considerable support from the Imperial Japan (as both the Japanese and the Indians had a common enemy—the British) and from the ethnic Indian population of Southeast Asia.

Meanwhile, in India, the activities of Subhash Chandra Bose

had forced the British to imprison him; however, he escaped to Germany in 1941. In 1943, he arrived in Singapore and took command of the INA, also known as the Azad Hind Army. Upon his leadership, there was a huge influx of volunteers to join the INA. It even had a separate all-women regiment which was named after Rani Lakshmi Bai of Jhansi.

Azad Hind Army's impact on India's freedom struggle was not military. It's the spirit of an Indian army comprising the prisoners of war formed on foreign soil and fighting for Indian freedom which galvanised the people. Though the Azad Hind Army had not been successful in accomplishing their goals, they did spread the spirit of nationalism.

By 1945, most of the INA soldiers were captured by the British and transported back to India.

Mohideen, after his days in the army, lived a simple life in Firozpur and did every little bit of thing he could do for Indian freedom by becoming a party member of the Indian National Congress. Kabir grew up seeing his father taking part in all the freedom movements. The thirst for a free nation had been instilled in him ever since he was a boy. His yearning to live in a free India was something that could never be uprooted from his heart.

Kabir came to Government Gordon College, Rawalpindi, in 1942 to pursue his B.S. in Political Science, along with his childhood friend Dayanand (Daya) from Firozpur. Daya was more of an amiable nerd who was clean shaven with round spectacles with parted and neatly combed hair. He was, for the most part, a shy person who took his share of time to observe before striking a conversation.

Daya and Kabir had been classmates since Class-1. Practically, they had houses on the same street and celebrated every possible festivity together from Diwali to Ramadan. Daya's father,

Bhattacharya was a priest at a local temple in Firozpur. Daya grew up hearing all the ancient stories that his dad would tell him every night to put him to sleep.

They also had a small piece of land where they grew wheat and paddy. Daya would help his parents during the harvest season. Sometimes, even Kabir would join the trio in the process. Every year, after taking the harvest for household consumption, not much would be left as surplus; nevertheless, they managed to make a modest living out of the small-scale reserve they had garnered. Daya grew up as a responsible child, being aware of his family's shortcomings right from his childhood, which made him prepare for his college entrance well in advance, and subsequently, clear through it.

The two friends at the same time made it to the prestigious Gordon's college at Rawalpindi after months of preparation together.

Kabir and Daya met Ibhrahim (Ibhu) on their first day of college. He was the last one to enter the class, and looked unbothered despite being late for 15 minutes. He had an athletic body and a playful smirk. He would sit on the last bench of class and make everyone around him comfortable with his jokes and by the way of his talking.

Kabir and Ibhu were united by their love for hockey. They would stay back after college and play for hours at the college ground. Daya would come to them as a saviour during the exam days, and soon, the trio became inseparable.

Ibrahim was from a small town called Sohawa near Rawalpindi. During weekends, Kabir and Daya would stay at Ibhu's house. Everyone who knew them understood that this was the kind of friendship that would stay till the end of time.

March 30, 1943

Daya had been in love with Laxmi Sehgal, his batchmate for almost a year. That day, he finally decided to ask for her hand in marriage and went to the Rawalpindi market to get some flowers. Kabir had been there in all of Daya's ups and downs. There was nothing Daya could do in his life without Kabir knowing it. He made sure of Kabir's presence that day.

The sun was beginning to set when they reached the market. It was bustling in its peak hour, flooded with hawkers trying their best to sell the flowers. The myriad colours and wonderful aroma of the flowers filled every nook and corner of the market.

While Daya was looking for flowers to gift his woman, Kabir found a small shop selling the best red roses in Rawalpindi, but it was not the roses that caught Kabir's eye. It was the girl behind those roses.

She was young and full of life, wearing a bright red kameez lustrous, pitch-black, braided hair. Her earrings went back and forth as her head nodded with a microdot red bindi at the centre of her forehead. It was like as if she almost camouflaged with those red roses.

There was something about her that Kabir couldn't help but gaze at, and he wondered whether she would notice him at all, which, by the way, she did.

Kabir was 6-feet tall with deep-set, calming eyes, the kind of eyes which would do all the talking; the lips seldom moved. He had an untamed, shiny goatee, bristly eyebrows accentuated by a sculpted jaw, muscled shoulders, and a dusky skin tone complementing all those features.

Maybe it was destiny that brought them together or the whole of the universe conspired in such a way that their paths would cross that day. Since then, there's been no looking back.

One wouldn't call it love at first sight; it was more like love at 'first vibe' for Kabir. The energy that she radiated and the mythical pull she exerted was too strong for him to resist. Kabir couldn't take his eyes off her. He kept going to her shop every morning just to get roses to gift her in the evening, and occasionally, he would strike a conversation with her.

He did this every other day until she finally said yes. Though Kabir had liked her ever since he saw her, his love grew only when they started spending time with each other. Everything about her, her likes, her interests just blew his mind.

It was Daya who wanted to establish his lady love that day, but the Gods brought Bhavna to Kabir. Bhavna was from a traditional Hindu family, residing in Rawalpindi. She was an artist by passion and a responsible daughter who also helped her father—a flower vendor at the market—early in the mornings and after college hours. Her life revolved around books, paintings (she had a special craze for oil paintings), and stars. Like any true artist, her imagination knew no boundaries. Kabir always knew she was a woman who belonged to a different era.

Kabir would often sneak to Bhavi's attic for a moonlight tryst, and there, they would lay breathing in each other's scent and reach out to the moon and the stars through the small vent on the roof. Bhavi had this obsession with the space and constellations ever since her childhood. She would draw different constellations in air with Kabir's hand and point out all the stars. Her favourite one was Sirius—the brightest star in the night sky. She even told him once, 'Kabir... you know... the Sun's rays take approximately few minutes to reach the surface of the earth, which means, if the Sun dies at this moment, it will take us minutes for us to even know... If this was the case for the Sun... imagine the stars! The stars that you are seeing today are the ones that existed hundreds of years ago.'

'A hundred years ago? Really?'

'Yeah... that is how much the light from the stars would take to reach us traveling continuously for years.' Her face shone brightly as she explained it to Kabir.

Their love for each other grew stronger with each passing day. They spent quite a lot of time together during their college days until that one day when Bhavi's father finally came to know about their relationship.

They got married despite all the false reasons in the world. Kabir's father played a significant role in convincing Bhavi's father and all their relatives with a promise that Bhavi would never be forced to convert to Islam and can always revere the God she believes in.

Chapter Two

A STAR IS BORN

August 14, 1947

11:58 p.m.

Rawalpindi

It was nearing 12, and the two greatest events in Kabir's life were about to happen. He knew that on the other side, his homeland was going to come to life at the stroke of midnight; India was all geared up to celebrate her long-awaited independence.

Kabir had settled in Firozpur with Bhavi after their marriage and had come to Bhavi's home at Rawalpindi only for her childbirth. He missed his homeland. More than that, he missed witnessing the smile on his father's face when he finally got to see the tricolour flag unfurl, but the havoc in Pakistan had already begun.

Communal riots slowly started breaking out in the outskirts of the town. It was aimed at the Hindu population and the people who wanted to move to India once the boundary line had been announced. The two countries that seemed to be prepared for freedom were not prepared for the partition and its aftermath.

India before Partition

14th August 1947. Pakistan got its independence while India got its independence a day later, on August 15, at midnight.

Bhavna gathered all her vigour and pushed the baby out one last time.

Devi Ma was ready to receive the baby with a piece of cloth and asked the maids to give pressure on her uterine fundus. The moment of relief came when the baby's head was finally out, and Devi Ma pulled the rest of the body. She witnessed the little one come to life and cut the umbilical cord. At that moment, there was no pain. All the pressure had gone at once. Devi Ma went near Bhavna and told her, 'She has Kabir's eyes...'

Bhavna was emotionally all over the place. Devi Ma wrapped the baby in a fresh piece of cloth and cleared the nose and mouth of the secretions while the baby was still giving a shrieking cry.

She also called Kabir inside and handed him the child. Kabir held his child for the first time and watched her quietly without uttering a word. His eyes brimming with tears, he stood speechless and went near Bhavna, sensing something gripping him right under his chest wall. He had never felt like this before.

The baby was trying to clasp his shirt with her pink, sodden fingers. There were tears, many tears. Three of them were having their moment together, while Devi Ma was busy pulling out the placenta. She gently pulled the remaining end of the cord, carefully twisting it and making the placenta slowly slide out. She then inspected for any cervical tear and then packed her vagina with a sterile cloth. Devi Ma always made sure she handled even the postpartum period with utmost care.

Kabir looked at Bhavna's face which was alit with adoration. She looked fatigued but gratified. A much stronger feeling took over her. He wiped out the beads of sweat on her forehead and reached out to tuck the strands of hair that were out of place. He then planted a kiss on her forehead and the other on the new-born. A kiss had never been so meaningful.

Before she was born, they had many a time fought on what they would name her. Kabir always thought it was going to be a boy. But that day, holding her close to his heart, amidst all the chaos of independence, Kabir couldn't help but call her "Indya".

That was the most beautiful name Bhavna or anybody else at that moment could think of, and thus, on the midnight of 14th August 1947, both India and Indya were born.

In the backdrop, tension arose on what were rumoured to be the borderlines. Nobody was sure where the boundary line was going to fall exactly.

August 17, 1947

Rawalpindi

Two days later, on August 17, the Radcliffe's boundary line that was to divide India and Pakistan was announced. Sir Radcliffe was a British lawyer who was entrusted with the daunting task of dividing India. That was the first time he had come to India and was nominated as the Chairman of the Boundary Line Committee. As irrational as it may sound, he had no idea of the Hindu-Muslim tensions that existed, or rather, had been developed as a result of the 'divide and rule' policy of the British for years.

The Muslim majority Baluchistan and Sindh province went entirely to Pakistan. However, Punjab and Bengal had an equal mix of Hindus, Sikhs, and Muslims. So, the line had to pass right through Punjab and Bengal. It went across roads, railways, farmlands, schools, power stations, and water systems recklessly, sending shock waves across the nation.

Those two states were to be hit the most because of this line. The

India after Partition

line established West Pakistan to the west of Punjab and East Pakistan to the east of Bengal.

The Hindus and Sikhs from the other side of the line had to leave their houses, lands, and all their properties to cross the line and reach India. Likewise, countless Muslims from the Indian territory crossed the line to enter Pakistan just to safeguard their lives. The announcement of the boundary line had spawned communal violence targeted against the opposite religion.

Millions of people migrated by walk, rails, or bullock carts, or by whatever means they could afford to. They took everything they could lay hold on. The old and the disabled were tied to long poles and carried by men. Soon, the trains were jam-packed. After filling their insides, many thronged on their roofs, while some hung outside with the bare support of doors and windows. The agitation was severe enough that people would kill each other just to get a space on the trains.

Kabir and Bhavna were perplexed. They had no idea what to do and where to go with a new-born baby in hand and the mother, who was still not out of post-partum.

While they were to decide which country to stay, Bhavna's father, who had gone to the market that evening, was struck in a violent mob clash. A few Muslims from that area had come together and hunted down every Hindu they came across. Bhavna's father was severely beaten up and thrashed and succumbed to death even before Kabir could arrive.

Bhavna was devastated. Kabir was fully aware that no amount of consolation would be of any help to her. Losing her father too soon was not something she had anticipated. More than the loss, the fact that he was killed by his own fellowmen with whom he had lived all these years was unacceptable.

Kabir knew these riots targeted against the Hindus were escalating at a much higher speed than they had contemplated.

Kabir felt, in his heart, that it was time to take Bhavna and Indya with him across the border by all means.

After conducting the funeral rites for Bhavna's dad, garnering all their spirits, the family decided to leave Rawalpindi that night.

Chapter Three

LEAVING EVERYTHING BEHIND

Devi Ma had packed a few maternal and new-born essentials along with some blankets, roti, and water, while Kabir managed to arrange as much money as he could. They had planned to get to Daya's house in Gujarkhan, around 60 kilometres away from Rawalpindi, and then decide on the whole crossing borders together.

They were all set to leave Rawalpindi in the morning of August 18 along with Kaala, Bhavi's pet dog. Kaala was an Indian Mastiff with almond eyes and an ebony velvet coat, weighing 60 kilos with canines that could pierce even the hardest of timber. He was rescued by Daya and Kabir from an illegal dogfighting contest in the suburbs of Rawalpindi.

Kaala, locally known as the Bully Kutta, were mostly raised for these despicable clashes. He was left on the streets by his owner with bruises all over his body and a lacerated wound near his jaw. It has been three years since his rescue, and if not for Kabir, he would have bled to death.

August 18, 5:50 a.m.
The first rays of the sun were beginning to fall. The air was still,

and the streets were quiet. Rawalpindi hadn't woken up yet. Kabir loaded their baggage in a neighbour's truck who was relocating within Pakistan and had graciously agreed to drop them on the way at Gujarkhan.

The stories about the trains from India loaded with the corpses of Muslims reaching Lahore had already reached their ears. Not a single person came alive from India to Pakistan on that train. Kabir was a realist; he knew that the avalanche had only begun. He told Bhavi that it was not going to be an easy journey and insisted on carrying only the most indispensable items with them.

Bhavi still hadn't recovered from her father's death, not to mention giving birth to Indya. She was both mentally and physically worn out.

But she was also aware that they were left with no other choice.

That morning, before leaving the house, the only thing persistent on her mind was to take Indya safely to India.

For one last time, before leaving, Devi Ma reminded them about the dos and don'ts of handling a new-born. Although Bhavi did her best in convincing Devi Ma to go along with them to India, she was resolute.

These were the words uttered by Devi Ma: 'This is where I was born, this is where all these years I had brought new ones to life, this is my homeland and I'm never leaving it.' With those words, she gave her final parting kisses to the baby and hugs to Bhavi with tears in her eyes rolling down her cheeks.

The truck slowly moved, and Bhavna stared at the crossroads of her street, wondering if that was the last time that she would get to see her hometown. She had lived there for 23 years. That's where she had done her schooling, spent the delightful days of college, met Kabir, and held her child for the first time. Above all, her house was the only space filled with memories of her mother. Now, she was leaving them, leaving all of them, forever.

Other than the most requisite items, Bhavna had also packed a portrait of her father and a dupatta that belonged to her mother. That was all she could take on their journey while leaving everything else behind.

Imagine if the country you live in right now gets divided into two countries, and suddenly, you are an alien in your own country. And if you need to travel to the other country for your survival, you need to leave behind your home, land, your friends, neighbours, and all that you have ever had since childhood. Even if you are taking all the things that you have owned, you wouldn't have any place to keep them in your country. You are going to be homeless for a certain period of time, or maybe, even for a lifetime. We don't know anything for sure. You can carry only the things that are of supreme importance to you. This was the situation of the 10 to 20 million people who were displaced across the lines after independence.

They reached Gujarkhan at noon. Daya was waiting to receive them. A much-needed old friends' reunion happened there. Daya and Laxmi had married 4 years ago and had settled in Gujarkhan with their 3-year-old son, Abhimanyu.

They were residing in a Hindu majority area. It was comparatively a safer place indeed. Kabir made sure that he visited Daya's family at Gujarkhan often.

Daya looked so much different now compared to his college days with a short moustache, a kumkum tilak at the centre of his forehead, and a white shirt tucked inside his loose, grey pants with sleeves folded up to the elbows.

Daya was such a compassionate and loved person in college. He was a disciplined and studious kid who would not sleep during his exam days. He had been the only reason why Kabir and Ibrahim had managed to pass their exams during their initial years in the college. He never broke any rule that the college imposed on them. His only weaknesses, rather his greatest strengths were his two dearest friends, Kabir and Ibrahim. Both would drag him into all their mischievous happenings. Despite all these, Daya would trust them with his life.

Kaala, on seeing Daya, got off the truck and hopped on onto Daya and started to lick him. The excitement was evident with Kaala wagging his tail, jumping up and down, and circling Daya. Daya reciprocated all the love that was showered on him, only that on his side, there was this anxious foreboding of what awaited them.

As Kabir got down with Indya, Daya lifted her for the first time and kissed her palms when she reached out to him. Laxmi hurriedly came running down the house, took the child in her arms, and exclaimed, 'Bhavi... she is just like you!'

'Thank the Lord she is not you, Kabir,' said Daya with a light chuckle.

'But she has my eyes, man,' replied Kabir as he gave a pat on his shoulders, and they hugged each other.

'It's good to see you Daya... we came to Rawalpindi together from Punjab, and now, we are going to leave together,' said Kabir with grief written all over his face.

Abhimanyu (Abhi), on seeing Kabir, came running towards him. He would call him *"Kabi paapa"*. Kabir was like a godfather to Abhi. Abhi loved listening to stories, and whenever Kabir visited him, he would tell him stories of Ashoka, Chandragupta Maurya, Alauddin Khilji, and other historical personalities.

'The story of Kohinoor' was Abhi's favourite story. He must have heard it 100 times and it never tired him to listen to it whenever Kabir visited them.

Bhavna put Indya to sleep and helped Laxmi in the kitchen. The two ladies, while chopping onions, discussed each of their experiences from their postpartum periods and Laxmi's sagacity on overcoming that phase with ease lit a spark of hope inside Bhavi's exhausted heart.

For dinner, Laxmi prepared vegetable pulao with all the remaining vegetables she had in her kitchen. It had been a week since they stocked up their groceries as it was not easy these days to get supplies. Almost all shops in Gujarkhan had either been closed or destroyed, and most of them had even been set on fire.

When Kabir revealed to Daya and Laxmi what had happened to Bhavi's father at Rawalpindi, they felt really sorry for her and made sure to not bring his topic at any cost and remind Bhavi of his death.

Placing the food before the family, Laxmi began, 'We need to vacate this house tomorrow morning. We aren't safe here anymore, and our neighbours have been vacating ever since the boundary line was announced. It will not be long until they've all gone.'

'Moreover, they are targeting Hindus all over Pakistan. Particularly violence is spewed on Hindus who had decided to leave the country. They are going to kill us someday or the other, so we might as well try crossing the border,' said Daya. Everyone agreed with what Daya said.

Deep down, they had accepted the fact that the chances of dying while relocating were extremely high.

'But can we cross the border ourselves safely? Somebody must help us,' Kabir responded.

'Ibhrahim might be able to guide us through. He has connections all over the country and he will definitely know a safe route,' Daya explained.

Ibhrahim was residing in Sohawa, which was around 30 kilometres from Gujarkhan. To get near the border, one must cross

Sohawa. Sohawa once used to be a Muslim neighbourhood which had now turned into a hub of communal riots. It all depended on Ibhu to show them a safer route, so that the families could leave the country safely.

Daya revealed to Kabir that a few of the Hindus from Pakistan, who wanted to enter India, had planned to enter India through Kartarpur with the help of the local Sikhs. He added that they had even planned to assemble on August 22 at 2 p.m. at the Gurdwara Darbar Sahib on the side of the newly created Pakistan. From there, they would cross the border to enter Dera Baba Nanak on the Indian side. Both the destinations were only 5 kilometres away from each other, and the majority of the residents were Sikhs on both the sides, who had promised to help them cross the border safely.

Kartarpur: The Kartarpur corridor is now a visa-free border and a religious corridor connecting the Gurdwara Darbar Sahib in Pakistan with the border in India. The crossing allows the devotees from India to visit the Gurdwara in Kartarpur, which is around 4.7 kilometres from the border on the Pakistan side without a visa. Earlier, the Sikh pilgrims from India had to travel to Lahore, which is a 125-kilometre journey (even though people on the Indian side of the border can physically see the Gurudwara Darbar Sahib from their end) and from Lahore, they had to travel all the way to Kartarpur.

'The Sikhs keep their word, and you know it,' was something Daya said to Kabir in a serious tone. Even before the words came from Daya's mouth, Kabir knew that they could be trusted.

After discussing the crossing, both the families sat together to break the tension in the air. Daya began narrating a story from their college days. Kabir often mentioned "their road trip to Srinagar" to Bhavi, saying that those days were the most memorable days of college life. As Kabir began to narrate the story, his enthusiasm seeped into the rest of them.

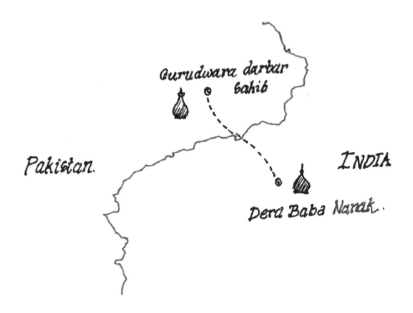

Chapter Four

THE TRIP OF A LIFETIME

It was the summer of 1944. Kabir and Daya had planned to spend their holidays at Rawalpindi that year. The three of them—Ibhrahim included—stayed together in a small, rented house near the college. That year, the Annual Rawalpindi Hockey Championship event was all set to take place.

Kabir and Ibhrahim were very good hockey players. Kabir was his team's captain. Then, the only two things that mattered to Kabir were Bhavna and hockey. That year as both of them were qualified to play in the tournament, they decided to play and won the trophy, too. But when the college re-opened after the summer holidays, the management suspended Kabir and Ibhrahim for not notifying them about the event despite winning the tournament.

They were suspended for 2 weeks, and official letters had been sent to their parents to notify them about the suspension. Kabir and Ibhu felt really bad. A suspension would lead to a lot of consequences from their parents' viewpoints.

Winning the trophy was one of the best things that had happened to them that year, but they never expected this kind of aftermath. During those two weeks, Daya had to leave for college while Kabir and Ibhu stayed back. The duo was getting sick of staying idle for days together, and the fact that their family has been notified made the situation worse.

'How can they suspend us even after winning the event?' they kept asking themselves many times and ranted about the doings of the college management.

After a week of loathing about the suspension, Kabir finally decided to spice these suspension holidays up with something that they had been wanting to do for a long time. He asked Ibhu whether they could go on an unplanned road trip like never before. Ibhu got excited and agreed instantly.

The two friends had always dreamt of travelling to the north of Rawalpindi, but they never had the chance to do so. Those areas were mostly hilly terrains, and transportation was the major problem there. That is why, this time, they decided to rent a motorbike from a family friend of Ibhu's and went out the following day to get a few supplies and an old map of the north-western part of India. They pooled all the money they had saved. That evening, when Daya came back from college, they told him about their plan.

Daya was a first bencher. Bunking classes and going on trips was not his cup of tea. He wouldn't say a yes to them despite being convinced to go along.

The next morning, Daya left early for college, and Kabir and Ibhu got ready for their trip with a half heart. They tied their supplies to the motorbike, locked their house, and as they were about to start their bike, Daya was standing right behind them.

Although he was the most obedient student in the college, he valued their friendship and loved spending time with them more than anything else.

'Were you ready to go on the trip without me? You jerks,' Daya grinned.

'We were never going without you,' Kabir chuckled happily and hugged him.

Even Ibhu who usually didn't show his inner emotions left the bike and joined the group hug and uttered, 'Our plan was to stop at the college first, to pick you up, you Bhattacharya.'

The three of them were all set, and they filled their bike's fuel tank. They planned to head to the North from Rawalpindi and not stop until they felt like they had reached their destination.

They had neither pre-planned any places that were to be visited nor had they meticulously worked out an itinerary; all they knew was that they were heading towards the North.

Ibhrahim drove the bike with Kabir at the tail end. Daya was sandwiched between the two, and bags of supplies were left to hang on both the sides. Thus, the three heads full of dreams started from Rawalpindi in the dawn of 17th May, unaware that they were headed for the trip of their lifetime.

The topography was mostly mountainous traversed by rivers and glistening lakes.

After an arduous journey with multiple halts and chai and samosas, they reached Taxila.

Taxila, also known as Takshashila, is one of the strategic and significant ancient cities and home to the earliest university (University of Takshashila). Also, it was the capital of Gandhara dynasty. Daya, who was well versed in Indian history, narrated the story of Gandhara to the other two.

Gandhara was one of the sixteen Mahajanapadas in the 4th century BCE, which played a crucial part in the Indian epic of Mahabharata. It was the birthplace of Gandhari (who was the mother of the Kauravas) and her brother, Shakuni, the crafty cunning maternal uncle of Duryodhana.

Upon Daya's request, they decided to visit Dharmarajika Stupa at Taxila, which is a Buddhist stupa built in the 2nd century CE by the Kushans to house the minute bone fragments of Buddha.

Kabir had always been keen to learn history. He found ancient Indian histories fascinating.

On their way, Daya also told them the story of how Shakuni became the reason for the greatest battle ever known to humans, Mahabharata, by just winning a game of rolling dice, later known as Ludo. Shakuni, though a physically disabled person, knew the right way to gybe any circumstance that came his way with his wisdom.

Ibhu kept yawning as Daya was narrating these stories to them.

They somehow reached Dharmarajika Stupa after multiple stops for directions.

The stupa was more than 1800 years old. Once, a renowned site was lying damaged and abandoned. It had been damaged by the Huna tribes from Central Asia in the 5th century CE. Under their reign, thousands of Buddhist monasteries around Gandhara were destroyed. This stupa was just one among them.

In the process of smashing down the Buddhist site, thousands of Buddhist monks were also killed and buried in and around the stupa.

Kabir loved archaeological sites. Stepping on to places that were centuries old gave him the kind of goosebumps which nobody could understand. He had brought with him a Kodak Brownie camera which was gifted by his father to him and began taking pictures of the ancient site.

Walking through the semi-ruined walls of the stupa, Kabir kept wondering why Indians were unable to relish the fullest legacy of our ancestors, be it any sect. He thought so, because with the advent of every new leader or idea that arose, either the religious structures present up until that time were destroyed or were made to lose their significance. By this way, not only did the particular religion that they wanted got propagated, but the history attached to it was also severed.

From Hagia Sophia to the Dharmarajika Stupa, every stone of those historical sites had layers of history embedded in them. Thousands of such structures around the world have all been lost and altered, particularly, in the name of religion.

He couldn't accept the fact that when a conqueror captures a country, he either destroys the significant religious buildings or converts them into a building of the religion that he wishes to propagate.

How can one disseminate the goodness of one religion when its genesis itself is a murder of another denomination? Oh, how many structures of historical significance have we missed because one ruler couldn't stand its very presence? he thought to himself.

Daya continued, 'Dharmarajika Stupa is the largest of all stupas in the Taxila region. The central large hemispherical mound that you see is the core stupa. The passageway between the main stupa and the other smaller stupas was used for practicing pradakshina— the ancient practice of walking around a holy site. And the row of small rooms that you see around the stupa are monastic cells.'

He added, 'The site was excavated before a few decades. The stupa was badly damaged and had been looted several times before its discovery.'

Kabir noticed two parts in the stupa complex. One was the stupa area consisting of the great stupa, and the other was the monastic area with monasteries from different periods. The top of the stupa mound was collapsed. The core stupa had a raised terrace around its base and four flights of steps, one at each of the cardinal points.

The place was deserted and there was hardly anybody except a tall guy in his twenties with a pair of round spectacles, who was clicking some pictures of the site, just like Kabir was. *Maybe he is a press reporter,* Kabir thought to himself.

Daya was the only reason they visited a site like this on their road trip. He was like a library of so many things. No doubt he was the topper of the class.

Hours went by strolling on the ruined site. Ibhu found these sites boring, and as he was starving, he dragged Kabir and Daya out of the place. They decided to have food at a small Dhaba and halted at Taxila that night. They stayed inside the premises of a local Vishnu temple, spread their blankets on the floor and used one of their bags as a headrest, staring at the sky.

It was a cold night and the guys had wrapped themselves up under their warm jackets. Within a few minutes, Kabir could hear Ibhrahim and Daya snoring. The very thought of the glory of those ancient civilisations and how it had moved him so much hovered in Kabir's mind. Slowly, he closed his eyes and slipped into sleep.

The next morning, Kabir woke up, and still hazy from last night's sleep, he found an extra blanket over him. Slowly, things came into focus, and he noticed Daya and Ibhu sleeping beside him and a third person standing near him, staring at the sculptures inside the temple.

Kabir stood up and splashed his face with some water. He looked for the guy. He saw him standing outside the temple premises, making a hot cup of tea, which he offered Kabir.

He recognised him. He was the same tall guy with a round pair of spectacles whom they had seen at the stupa. He was Vimal Adityan, a 6-feet tall, fair-skinned, curly-haired, handsome young man. He was wearing a loose, checked shirt with a black jerkin and a grey shawl covering his neck. From his looks, you could say that he was from a well-to-do family.

Kabir was hesitant at first, but as Vimal insisted on having tea, both of them sat together and enjoyed the sunrise over a hot cup.

The Vishnu temple was located on the edge of a small cliff, making way for a spectacular view of the sunrise. They had little chitchat about each other, and Kabir came to know that Vimal was the son of a minister from the court of Maharaja Hari Singh of Kashmir. He was a history graduate and an intern at ASI (Archaeological Survey of India). In his free time, took his bike and camera and set out, exploring new places.

That was the first time Kabir was hearing about ASI.

After an hour or so, Daya and Ibhu had woken up and joined them for tea. They say some people connect just like that, and so did Kabir and Vimal. All three of them liked Vimal very much, and since they didn't have a pre-planned itinerary, they decided to include Vimal with them in the trip.

Daya was more than happy to continue the trip with Vimal, and the only reason being that he could finally sit freely on the bike. Hours of being sandwiched between Kabir and Ibhu had made him tired. Vimal had come on his bike and Kabir switched bikes and sat behind Vimal.

After travelling for a few hours, and taking a few pitstops, they literally got lost among the woods. Roads became narrow and unpaved, the sun was about to set, but still, they couldn't find a place to halt and sleep that night. Therefore, they kept riding on their bikes in spite of the sunlight diminishing with every passing minute. Suddenly, the roads came to an end. They could see a small pathway leading from there on, yet treading would be very difficult with the motor bikes.

There were boulders on either side, and they could hear some hushing noise from far away. The guys decided to park their bikes aside and proceed on foot towards the direction of the noise.

At this point, the sun had already set, and darkness was mounting in. Within a few minutes, it became pitch dark. Kabir and Ibhu had to switch their torch lights on. Daya, who was following Ibhu, was the last one in the line. He soon changed his position and went next to Kabir, making Vimal and Ibhu walk behind. In this way, he felt that the probability of him being safe would be high. That was Daya! He was a kid at heart.

Other than him, all the three men were equally excited about exploring the wilderness. Neither the wild darkness nor the hushing noise could scare them. They were walking on a small pathway sufficient for one person to walk at a time. It seemed pretty sure that the path might have been made by people traversing through these routes frequently. They continued their journey forward and hoped to find something to pass the night on.

Daya found it difficult to climb up, as the further they went, the path kept inclining and the noise became louder and clearer. Clear enough to listen, but at the same time, not loud enough to figure out what it exactly was.

They found the vegetation getting scanty and were able to feel the chillness beneath their outfits. Kabir was the first to witness it. It was an astounding waterfall, glimmering white in the moonlight, gushing with tonnes of water, thundering and plunging deep into the ground. The chill breeze and millions of water droplets began hitting them on their face.

The petrichor was so fresh and alluring. The waterfall kept gurgling as it travelled along its course, standing more than a hundred-feet tall and majestic. It tumbled down the hill so gracefully. A picture that looked so chaotic was rather more calming to the four men who came across it by chance. It wasn't every day that you stumbled upon a waterfall that massive out of nowhere.

After taking in the magnificence of the beauty that they had witnessed just then, Kabir noticed a small mandap-like structure a few hundred metres away. It seemed like a remnant of an old temple.

The friends decided to spend the night there and began walking towards it with only the moonlight as their guiding source. They managed to get inside the mandap without their clothes getting wet. Quickly, they prepared a makeshift bed and decided to crash right away. Nevertheless, all four of them could not sleep despite the wearisome travel the whole day. Their eyes wouldn't shut as they were too delighted after seeing what was right in front of them.

They began chatting about life, love, friendships, and freedom. It went on and on for hours together. There was something about that place that they just couldn't sleep that night. It was as if they belonged there. It felt meaningful. It was their calling.

Kabir began narrating his love story, how he saw Bhavi for the first time and his plans on marrying her in the following years. Kabir showed Vimal a picture of Bhavi which he had saved in his wallet. Daya, for his part, shared his love story. He explained about his love, Laxmi, and how he wanted to bring up their children in the future.

Ibhu shared his childhood days with his sister Raziya, and Vimal told everyone a few of the interesting things that happened in the court of Raja Hari Singh. He narrated a story of the two groups of villagers who went to the Raja's court for justice.

The first group was the wealthy educated Hindus who wanted to build a temple on the outskirts of the village. The second group was the illiterate and poor Muslims, living on the outskirts of the village. They were asked to vacate their place and live elsewhere.

The men from the Hindu group were close associates of Raja himself. So, he could neither say no to them nor leave the Muslims with injustice. If he ended up saving the houses of Muslims, then he would lose the support of the wealthy men which was vital for him as a ruler of the state. They had previously made various donations to the court. Meanwhile, he was upset about seeing the plight of the poor Muslim men. They were farmers and cowmen, and their livelihoods were tied up to the place that they were living on for years.

The Raja finally ended up nodding yes for the temple construction with no other option left. However, he agreed to allow the Muslim men a separate place in their community where they could begin from scratch.

This led to resentment and angered the Muslims and that was the beginning of the hundreds of rebellions that were to follow, orchestrated by the Muslims against the King stating his unfairly rule against them. Despite being the majority population of the state, Raja's court had predominantly Hindus. So, they had nobody else to voice out their issues.

Even though Raja tried his best in making both the Hindus and the Muslims co-exist in harmony, all his attempts went in vain as the anger and resentment festered inside them. They formed groups and elected their leaders and had been causing great trouble to Raja's rule ever since this problem. They conducted frequent campaigns and rebellions against Maharaja, leading to a constant fuss at his court.

Daya and Kabir slowly drifted to sleep in the midway of the story that Vimal was narrating. But Ibhu couldn't sleep, and he went deep into this story and even asked a little more than a hundred doubts all that night to Vimal on how Muslims were treated in the state he lived.

He just couldn't accept the fact that Muslims suffered only because they did not have proper representatives to voice out the problems they were facing as minorities. Even Vimal agreed with Ibhu, stating that they did not have proper representatives. Ibhu ended the hours-long conversation saying that he wished he could do something about it.

In the morning, Kabir was the first to wake up to the sound of the gushing waterfall in the background. He kept staring at the water flowing calmly. The distinct bluish hue that it possessed made it look as if it was straight out of a painting.

Vimal in spite of sleeping late woke up anyway as the sun began to spread its rays right on his face. He interrupted Kabir, saying, 'It's more beautiful in the morning, isn't it?'

Kabir replied, 'Oh, yes! Did you look at that colour?'

'Yes. Looks magical. Are you thinking what I am thinking right now?' said Vimal, chuckling lightly.

And the two men dove into the plunging pool and stayed in the water until Ibhu and Daya joined them. The water was cold, yet the experience was once in a lifetime as the men lazily floated along the currents of the water.

The water body seemed like a world of its own and had an offbeat charm. It was well tucked inside the middle of a forest, untouched and away from the crowds.

After spending quite some time on the waterfall, the men half-heartedly packed their bags and left the place. And this time, Vimal would not reveal their next destination. After days of travelling and sleeping wherever they found places, tiredness slowly seeped in. They began missing their home.

Their ride that day was one of the most beautiful journeys they had ever taken. Breathing in the misty air, their heart synchronising with the streaming rivers on either side of the roads, the sun-kissed snow-capped mountains gave an amazing view; fields of saffron, and the orchards of apple gave the air a distinct smell, and everything together gave a sense of peace and bliss that words couldn't explain.

Kabir had never seen anything more beautiful than this place. Every frame was picturesque. The sun was about to set, and Vimal halted in front of a bungalow. He got off his bike and welcomed the three men inside his home.

That night's halt was at Vimal's home in Srinagar, and that marked the end of their once-in-a-lifetime trip.

The three entered Vimal's house, quiet and surprised by the sheer grandeur of the place. They were welcomed by his mom who served them a warm cup of Kahwa tea. Her hospitality made them feel at home instantly. Vimal showed them the whole place and convinced them to stay at their guest room that night. The house had a lavish garden in the front. There were many servants, merely one for each

work. That was the first time Ibhu, Kabir, and Daya had been to a rich household like that.

Dinner was quite a spread with Kashmiri kebabs, meatball curry, and pulao. The steaming kebabs were mouth-watering, and Kabir and Ibhu loaded their tummies with them. Daya, who was on the other side of the table, could not stand the smell of the kebabs. He closed his eyes, trying his best to avoid seeing them most of the time. He had vegetable pulao in peace while Kabir and Ibhu teased him to taste the kebabs for once. He ran away from the table and ended up having his dinner on the stairs.

At night, they caught up on all the sleepful nights that they had missed for the past few days. The next morning, Vimal took Kabir to his father's room and showed him the pictures that were framed on the wall. The one where Vimal and his father were standing beside Raja Hari Singh was the one that caught Kabir's eye. Vimal narrated every story behind those pictures one by one.

Out of the three friends, Vimal somehow ended up liking Kabir the most for no particular reason. The liking just came quite naturally. They had the same outlook on life. And it felt as if they knew each other for a very long time.

Daya and Ibhu joined them in Vimal's father's room and Vimal knew it was time for them to leave. He had a camera set up in that room and the four friends took a picture together.

Before parting ways, Vimal took down his address on a paper and handed it to Kabir. They promised each other to stay in touch for the years to come and to go on more trips together in the future.

All good things come to an end, and so did their trip. Their journey home was rather boring, unlike their onward journey. All three were sad that they had to go back to their routine life at Rawalpindi.

While on the way back, somewhere near the outskirts of Rawalpindi, they came across a dog, a bully kutta brutally injured and bleeding to death. Kabir loved dogs. His heart couldn't just leave him there in such a pathetic state. He decided to take it with him to Rawalpindi.

That trip had been very important to all three of them. Each one of them found their callings after this trip. Daya documented their trip in their college year magazine. He ended his write-up with these lines:

'There are two kinds of people in this world:

Those who loves the sand, the sun, and the beach,

And those who love the mountains, clouds, and waterfalls.

And I definitely belong to the latter category.'

He got appreciated for his write-up and was even invited to his college's editorial committee. That was the beginning of his writing journey. After college, he decided to pursue his career in writing, and also, became the editor of a regional newspaper.

Kabir realised nothing excited him more than histories and ancient civilisations. Despite being a political science graduate, he decided to pursue his interests in archaeology and joined the Archaeological Survey of India (ASI).

He got a chance to work on an excavation project on the sites of Mohenjo-Daro. He eventually joined the team of the official photographers of ASI. He mostly travelled to historical sites and documented them. He was more than satisfied to get this job. He was content and led a simple happy life.

Ibhrahim came to know that all these days, politics was his only interest. He had strong views on how Islamic people were suppressed just because they were a minority. He respected his religion more than anything else. He realised he could only be content with a job that gave him a platform where he could fight for the rights of his people.

Although a true believer in Islam, he never put down any other religion. He was just strong about Islam. He even quit his studies to join the All-India Muslim League political party. After his college days, he became an influential person in the North-Western provincial regions of British India.

Chapter Five

THE DEPARTURE

August 19, 7 a.m.

Day 2

Just before they left for Sohawa, Kabir briefed them about the riots that had started spreading at a colossal rate. Even the places that were once safe were now booming with protests as tensions increased. Kabir, being aware that they could never travel this way, asked Bhavi and Laxmi to disguise themselves as Muslim women.

They changed into plain white Kameez with full sleeves. Kabir covered Bhavi's head with her dupatta, noticing the dark circles that had now formed under her once dreamy eyes.

Of all of us, she was hit the most, Kabir thought to himself.

He cupped her face with his hands. 'We are going to be in India in a few days.' Her eyes became moist as she held back her tears.

Laxmi and Bhavi did away their bindi, kumkum, bangles, and hid their mangalsutra. Kabir gave one of his *taqiyahs* (rounded cap traditionally worn by Muslim men) to Daya. They now resembled two Muslim families relocating within Pakistan.

The party loaded some packed food and a large container of water on Daya's bullock cart and started their journey. Kaala was going along with them on the road.

On their journey from Gujarkhan to Sohawa, they encountered a furious mob burning the Indian Swaraj Flag. After a few of them had left, Kabir tried to extinguish the fire set to the flag. A rioter, on spotting this, hurled a stone at him that got him bleeding. Before anyone could perceive what just happened, Kaala charged on the rioter, giving him no chance but to run.

Daya was able to manoeuvre the little time they had, managing to grasp Kabir and escape in their cart to Sohawa before the rioters gathered again. The stone had a sharp edge that pierced a few millimetres on Kabir's forehead. Equipped with nothing but bare essentials, Bhavi attempted to temporarily stop the bleeding by tightly wrapping a cloth around his head.

The route to Sohawa got more and more crowded as time passed by, and thousands of people hit the roads. The sight of all these people, who were once a part of this land, leaving everything behind and moving across the line just to safeguard their lives, made Bhavi realise that they were not the only ones undergoing this struggle. The presence of Indya in the cart managed to liven up the spirit of the members while the cart moved inch by inch in the scorching daylight.

After a monotonous, tiresome journey, they reached Ibhrahim's house by evening. Ibrahim's house was situated in a Muslim neighbourhood. As long as they kept their identities to themselves, they could be in a safe space. Nobody other than Ibrahim knew that all of them were Hindus with the exception of Kabir.

The last time Kabir and Daya had come to Sohawa was 3 years back. It had been a calm and serene locality. Today, it was menacing with communal activities.

Hundreds of people were on the road, forming small groups here and there. Some kept shouting slogans and carrying flags. They stared at the newcomers as their cart entered the street. Although disguised as Muslims, Daya felt like a herd of deer that had lost the way and entered a lion's territory. They stopped in front of Ibrahim's house as Kabir went inside to look for him.

Daya was reminiscent of the last time he had been in Sohawa.

It so happened that one year, during one of their Ramadan holidays, as Firozpur was hit by cyclones, Daya and Ibhrahim had no choice, but to stay back at Rawalpindi. Ibhu took both of them to his house in Sohawa. Ibhu was the kindest among the three of them. He had lost both of his parents at a young age and was raised by his elder sister, Raziya.

She took up the role of being a mother, a father, and a sister to Ibhrahim. She was everything to him. Raziya was a strong and patriotic woman who had even joined the Azad Hind Army in the all-women Rani Lakshmi Bai regiment. As Kabir's father was a member of the army, Kabir and Daya had huge respect for Raziya.

That year, during the eve of Ramadan, many activities were arranged in Sohawa. There were games, events, and the streets were all lit up. People hardly slept during those days. But that day, Daya, who usually got excited during festivities, seemed melancholic.

He hardly got involved in any of those events but spent the day sitting up all alone at the veranda of Ibhrahim's house, watching Kabir and Ibhu taking part in all the events. Raziya was also like a sister to Kabir and Daya.

While enquiring about what went wrong, Daya revealed to Raziya that as his parents who were farmers at Firozpur lost all their crops due to the cyclone that year. They could not even pay for his college fees that semester. The due date for the payment was after the Ramadan holidays. That kept bothering him.

Every time his parents would struggle to pay his fees, he made sure they somehow paid before the last date. But sadly, this year, he couldn't do anything.

Raziya consoled him by saying, 'Only situations like this shape you into a better person. You will grow up to know the value of money. Don't worry.' She also told him to meet his college superiors and ask some more time by explaining his family's condition.

'As you are an excellent student, trust me, they will understand your situation and give you some extra time,' she said.

Daya somehow got convinced. They all had their Ramadan dinner together, and Daya slept peacefully that night.

The day after the Ramadan holidays got over, Daya went to meet his college Vice Principal. In the administrative office, while they asked him the reason for wanting to meet the VP, he explained to them about his financial crisis.

The office staff checked the list, and to his surprise, he was told that his fee had already been paid that morning itself. Later that day, Kabir revealed that Ibhrahim had paid his fee by mortgaging Raziya's bangles.

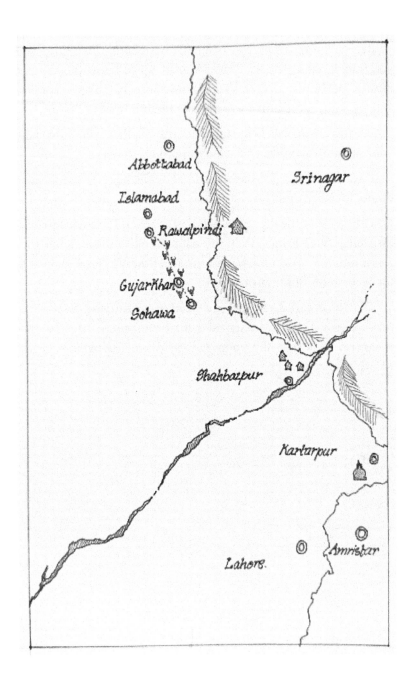

Chapter Six

THE STARRY NIGHT

August 19, 1947

Day 2

Kabir came out of the house with Ibhrahim.

The sight of his dearest friends disguised as Muslims took Ibhrahim by shock. 'What have you done to yourselves?' he exclaimed.

'We had no other option,' Daya said as he got down from the cart.

The three friends had a long embrace and Ibhrahim was more than happy to receive his friends along with their families to his home. Kabir decided to lodge at Ibhrahim's house that night and start their journey to Kartarpur the next day in the safest route possible with Ibhu's help.

Ibhrahim's house was his ancestral property, a decades-old, two-storey house with wooden balconies protruding out. As Bhavi entered the house, she could smell mildew. The walls were adorned with oil paintings and ceilings panelled with wooden planks.

Ibhrahim had asked Daya and Laxmi to stay in his room on the ground floor and Kabir and Bhavi to stay on the first floor.

Bhavi, being an aesthete herself, could not stop admiring those paintings. In the hall, there was a grand Islamic wall art with Arabic letters enclosed in a golden frame.

While taking the wooden stairs to the first floor, she noticed the paintings that were kept next to each other. The painting, "Impression sunrise" by Claude Monet, was hung but slightly tilted to one side. Bhavi tried to put it back on position, but it kept slipping again. Next to it was the beautiful "Red Vineyard".

When she entered her room, she stumbled upon "The Starry Night over the Rhone" by Vincent Van Gogh. She stood speechless, staring at the starry night, taken aback by its serenity.

'Raziya loves paintings,' Kabir interrupted as he placed their bags on one corner of the room.

'These paintings add so much life to this house. I wish we had paintings like these in our house, too,' says Bhavi.

'Of course, we'll get them. It's on me, don't you worry,' Kabir responded.

'I get a feeling that these paintings are communicating something... to us,' said Bhavi.

'Kabir... dinner is here,' Ibhrahim interrupted by shouting from the ground floor.

Kabir replied, 'We will continue talking after dinner,' and left the room. Bhavi fed Indya and put her to sleep to join them downstairs.

Ibhrahim had prepared quite a spread for them for dinner, and there was a lot of love, laughter, and banter quoting their college days as the three friends had come together after a long time.

After dinner, Abhimanyu began pestering Kabir for his favourite bedtime story, "The Kohinoor diamond". Kabir, who didn't have the heart to say 'no' to Abhi, lifted him with one hand, and said to Daya, 'Let him sleep with us tonight. I will tell him all the stories that he asks and put him to sleep,' squeezing his cheeks with fondness.

Abhi got excited and ran to Bhavi.

The three sat down on the divan kept inside their room as Kabir began narrating the story of Kohinoor. Bhavi looked intently at Kabir and was equally engrossed in the story as Abhi himself.

Kabir began,

'The Kohinoor diamond was first found in the Golconda mines of Kakatiya dynasty in Warangal. It was **Kakatiya** kingdom's most valued possession for years. When **Alauddin Khilji** conquered Delhi, he sent his General, Malik Kafur, to raid the southern Indian Kingdoms.

Malik Kafur looted the Kakatiya kingdom and even took their Kohinoor diamond with them. There was a curse on that diamond that whoever owned it would fall ill and eventually die. Soon after possessing it, Khilji got killed in a conspiracy.

The diamond was then passed on to the Mughals. **Shah Jahan**, mesmerised by its beauty, ordered his servants to build him a golden throne embedded with the most precious stones, gems, emeralds, and on the top of it, placed the Kohinoor.

The throne, so made, became the greatest throne ever made in Indian history and was named the **"peacock throne"**. It took 7 years just to build the extravagant throne, and it was more than twice as valuable as the Taj Mahal at that time.

The throne was held by the Mughal Kings, until that one day when an Iranian ruler **Nadir Shah** looted Delhi and took their peacock throne with him. He carved out the Kohinoor diamond from it and he was the one who named it the Kohinoor, which in Persian meant "mountain of light".

As he was curious to find the value of the diamond at that time, his goldsmiths, after days of calculating, came up with an answer. If a strong soldier threw five stones, each one in all the four directions, and the fifth one up in the air, and if a pyramid was drawn by connecting all those points, and even when the entire pyramid was filled with gold, the value of that gold would be lesser than the Kohinoor.

Nadir Shah, astonished by this answer, carried the Kohinoor with him wherever he went. It soon drove him crazy, and he ended up being killed by his own men who conspired against him.

After him, it was passed on to the Afghans, and then, from there to **Maharaja Ranjit Singh**, the founder of the Sikh empire in return for saving the Afghan prince's life. Ranjit Singh, on knowing the value of the diamond, grew paranoid regarding its safety. He wore it in his turban during festivals, and whenever he travelled, he placed the diamond on a basket and carried it on a camel. He even made 30 such camels carrying empty baskets move along. Only his most trusted person knew which camel carried the diamond... but the curse did not spare Ranjit Singh also...

'Abhi?' Kabir called.

'He dozed off when Nadir Shah got hold of the diamond,' Bhavi giggled.

'And were you listening the whole time?' Kabir asked. His eyes wrinkled near the corners.

'Yeah. I was... and what happened to the diamond now? Who owns it?' Bhavi questioned.

'The Queen of Britain owns it. Let's leave the diamond for now, and you come over here,' said Kabir, pulling Bhavi closer. The room was now brimming with romance.

For the past few days, they had not got much time to spend with each other. Bhavi noticed that blood was still oozing out from the wound on his forehead and asked him to get to a doctor as soon as possible.

Kabir opened the window and a gush of cool breeze entered. He gently brushed Bhavi's hair and asked, 'How are you feeling now? Has the pain relieved?'

'It's better. But I need some time to rest. I'm looking forward to reaching India soon,' she replied.

'We are going to India before long. But it's just that we left most of your belongings back in Rawalpindi. I'm really sorry that we had to leave everything behind in that way,' Kabir responded.

'I have taken the things that matter to me the most. You are here. Indya is here. Look, what I have with me.'

Bhavi took a book out of her bag and asked Kabir to open it. He recognised that book. It was the first thing that he had ever gifted Bhavi. It was a hundred-year-old Quran, gifted by Kabir's grandfather to him. He had treasured it for all those years and had gifted it to Bhavi.

And when he opened it, he found an old red rose, now almost rusty brown but well pressed and preserved in between pages.

'It's the rose that you gave me on the very first day,' said Bhavi.

Even while leaving all her stuff behind, she had carried the Quran with the preserved flower inside it. Kabir adored these little things and moments Bhavi took care to remember and create.

He scooped her into his arms and whispered, 'You are the best thing that has ever happened to me. I cannot imagine how my life would have drifted if I hadn't met you. I love you. Bhavi.'

She wrapped her arms around him and hugged him tightly. Suddenly, she felt pain in her groin. The pain usually came in waves. If hugs could heal, she wouldn't leave him for days.

He patted and watched her slowly fall asleep.

After some time, around 11 o'clock, after Bhavi had slept, Kabir went outside to see Ibrhahim. He asked Ibhu whether he knew any doctor nearby.

As his family doctor was only two streets away, Ibrahim said, 'It's better if we go to him immediately as you might need a suture or two on your forehead.'

Kabir went upstairs and informed Bhavi while she was still half-asleep. She couldn't sleep well that night as she had fragments of bad dreams of Jatayu being brutally injured by Ravana while abducting Sita.

Kabir chained Kaala to the pillar outside the main door at the veranda and both of them started walking to the doctor's residence.

At the Doctor's house

12:45 a.m.

The doctor examined his wound after giving a wound wash and told him that the wound needed to be sutured. The doctor proceeded with the sutures. In the meantime, Kabir and Ibrahim started discussing their families.

Kabir asked Ibhu about Raziya whom he had admired.

Kabir added, 'She is the boldest woman I have ever seen.'

'Yeah... she was,' Ibhu smiled wistfully.

'Was? Where is she now?'

'She is no more.'

Kabir froze and kept staring at him. 'What do you mean, "she is no more"? You said she joined the Army.'

'The Hindus killed her.'

Kabir stood in aghast, unable to coin words to speak, and Ibrhahim began to narrate.

In the army, Raziya used to wear a hijab along with her army uniform, which many religious Hindus made fun of and didn't tolerate. One day, they crossed their limits and assaulted her. They gave her the choice of wearing either the army uniform or the hijab. Any at cost, she wouldn't give up her hijab. She stood there, tall, and proud, conveying to them how both her religion and country were equally important to her.

Those men ripped her hijab off in front of everyone and even tried to take her uniform off. She resisted initially, and tried to push them off, but it was of no use. It was one against four.

This incident had festered deep inside her head. She couldn't digest men laying hands, outraging her modesty by taking out her hijab in front of everyone. She paid for it with her life.

That was when Kabir noticed that something was wrong with Ibhrahim. He was not the same. His eyes turned red, full of tears, and anger. It quickly struck Kabir how full of emotions he was and asked him whether he had revealed to anybody about them staying at his house.

'Kabir... you are two streets away and safe here with me.'

Chapter Seven

THE BETRAYAL

Kabir felt a jolt through his heart. He grabbed Ibhu's neck and almost choked him. When the terror struck and the doctor called out for help, he left Ibhu and hurried to his house.

Ibhrahim's House

August 20, 1:45 a.m.

The gates were open, the front door slightly broken and ajar. Kabir gathered his spirits and rushed inside as a great tremor overtook him. In the hall, he found Daya lying down with his throat cut open amidst a pool of blood. As he went near him, for the first time, he smelt the human blood.

There he was, his dearest friend, lying motionless. He turned his head away and noticed the walls having blood prints on them. As difficult it was, he could visualise Daya fighting for his life, the visuals coming right before his eyes.

He turned towards Laxmi lying in the bed in her room. She lay motionless, too. Kabir went near her, only to notice that her face had

been disfigured and swollen, her eyes bloodshot, still open with a terror in her eyes that could not be put into words.

It took some time for Kabir to realise that she had been raped and stabbed to death. She had multiple stab wounds all over her body. The mattress below her was soaked in blood and had turned into a dark, brick-red colour. He turned his face away as tears welled up.

The moment he thought of Bhavi, his heartbeats went arrhythmic.

Gathering the meagre life left in him, he raced to find Bhavi. He spotted the Islamic art on the hall spilt with fresh blood. While he took the stairs, he found Kaala whining to take his last breath. His head had been thrashed brutally and the blood oozing from his head dripped down the stairs.

He held Kaala for one last time, only to realise that he had just passed away. Tears already rolling down, he felt his throat tightening and heartbeats exploding up. All the paintings from the side walls had fallen and broken.

He ran upstairs to find Bhavi. The room was open, but the cot was empty. Bhavi and Indya were not there. Even Abhimanyu, who had been sleeping on the divan was not there. He scanned the room to check for any evidence of blood spill; there was nothing.

His world stopped for a second. He couldn't hold it any longer, fell on his knees and screamed at the top of his voice. There were two people whom he had treasured his whole life; one was laying down with his throat cut open and the other was nowhere to be found. A flood of uncontrollable tears gushed down his cheeks. He looked at his hands; they had the bloodstains of Kaala. He wiped down his tears, yet they didn't cease.

Kabir looked around. The walls of the room swirled; he was losing his balance. He took a deep breath and searched for anything he could find. Their bags lay as they were. He looked out through

the window and felt a chill, the room seemed colder than any winter he had experienced.

Something hit his foot on the floor, and he bent to notice. It was the Quran that he had gifted Bhavi. He lifted it with his blood-stained hands and thought how a few hours before Bhavi was holding it in her hands. He remembered the painting that Bhavi kept staring at the previous evening.

Something seemed odd. Further down the starry night painting, he found a sketch of a constellation. He recognised Orion's belt in it. He realised it must be Bhavi. She had drawn it on the wall. It was not there when they had entered the room that night. He wiped it with his fingers and noticed that it had been drawn on the wall with Kajal.

He remembered the nights they had spent together at the attic, gazing at each other most of the time, and at times at the stars, sometimes wondering which one was more magical. And it suddenly struck him that she could be hiding in the attic.

He searched for a staircase upstairs, but the doors were sealed from outside. He tried to break them open, but they didn't give away easily. He went downstairs and found a small dagger lying on the stairs. He picked it up and came back to the room. He emptied one of their bags and packed whatever he found important. At last, he packed the Quran, too. He knew how much Bhavi valued it. He put the bag on his shoulders and peeked outside through the windows.

He found planks of concrete sticking out through the walls. Without thinking for a minute, he jumped out of the window and landed on a block of concrete. He balanced himself and tried to climb above by holding on to the pipes that went vertically down from above. He struggled and somehow reached the attic. As he snuck inside, there she was.

Bhavna was there, having Indya tied on her shoulders by a sling that she had made with her dupatta. She held Indya in one hand and had tightly wrapped her other arm around Abhimanyu. Kabir, on seeing her, was finally able to breath freely then.

On seeing him, she could feel her throat closing up, as tears streamed down her face. He could feel the grief pouring out. It was evident from the look on her face. She was dripping in sweat and trembling with fear. Kabir hugged the three of them together. That was the moment she found her salvation. She grasped his hands and narrated all the events that happened after he had left.

August 20, 12:40 a.m.

Ibhrahim's house

Bhavi woke up with a jolt. She heard Kaala barking loudly. When she peeked out through the windows, she found around 5 to 6 men pounding the house door open with an axe and breaking into the house. They had knives and iron rods with them.

On seeing this, her heart began beating faster than ever. She looked back to find Abhimanyu on the couch and Indya on the cot. Both of them were peacefully asleep. In a few minutes, she heard the thuds and screams of Daya and Laxmi. She knew they were outnumbered. If she went downstairs right now, she would be helpless and exposed.

With trembling hands, she quickly made a sling and tied Indya onto her trunk. She closed Abhimanyu's mouth with a piece of cloth and lifted him. She could not go down the stairs. Even the door to upstairs was sealed.

She opened the windows and realised they could get out through that. By that time, she could hear Kaala charging at those men. His growls were louder than ever. She realised Kaala was somewhere near the stairs and quickly drew an Orion constellation with the kajal she had and managed to jump out of the window.

The pain that came with every step that she made carrying Indya and Abhi reminded her that it had been only a few days since her delivery. She knew that if she climbed down, they would know and follow her. So, she decided to climb above and reach the attic.

Standing on the verge of the plank, she quickly tossed Abhimanyu above and then dragged herself to the attic.

While trying to explain what was happening to Abhi, Indya woke and gave out a wail. Bhavi carefully pacified her and not knowing what to do or where to go next, she sat there only with the hope that Kabir would find them.

Attic, 2:30 a.m.

'You are a brave woman, Bhavi. Don't worry, I'm here now, and I'm not leaving you alone hereafter,' said Kabir, mollifying Bhavi.

That night, they decided they would only travel during the night and hide during the day. Kabir knew that he somehow should reach Kartarpur on August 22. That was their only safe chance for crossing the border.

Travelling in trains was the easiest but dreaded the most. Either the trains were blasted, or they reached the destination empty. They needed to get out of Ibhu's place as soon as possible as he knew that they might come in search of him.

Chapter Eight

THE ESCAPE

August 20, 4:30 a.m.

Day 3

It slowly began to drizzle. In a few minutes, thunder was booming outside, and rain began to pour heavily. Every drop of it hit the roof tile like bullets. The attic was leaking, and water started to stagnate around them. Bhavi held Indya in her arms, tightly wrapped around, and Kabir held Abhi.

Kabir tried to explain Abhimanyu that his parents were going back to their house in Gujarkhan since they had left some important belongings back there. 'And you get to stay with me and Bhavi to hear a lot of stories every day until they come back,' Kabir added.

The three-year-old, who was half asleep and didn't have a clue of what was going on around him, just nodded his head and fell asleep again. When he was asleep, Kabir and Bhavi had a conversation, and they decided to bring him up as their son. 'He came to our room last night for hearing his favourite story, and from this day, he is going to spend the rest of his life with us,' Kabir whispered. 'You always wanted a boy first, didn't you? Here he is,' Bhavi said as she pressed her forehead against him and wiped his tears.

After an hour of heavy downpour, the rain stopped for a while. Kabir decided to get out of the attic before the sun rose. He carried his bag and tried to look outside the attic. It was still dark. People had not come out yet. He realised that this was the right time to escape.

He decided to get down first and managed to balance himself and got Abhi as Bhavi gave him to Kabir. Holding Abhi in one arm, he extended his other hand to get Indya. He got hold of the sling and slowly Indya wiggled her arms. Kabir looked at her, still asleep, sticking out her tongue. He carefully tied her around his torso tightly.

He reached out his other hand to Bhavi, and she jumped down cautiously. To Bhavi, this time, it was easier as Kabir was beside her. They slowly made their way down and reached a nearby house's roof top. They climbed down the roof, tiptoed with utmost care, and continued walking in the rain, unaware where to stay.

It began to pour again. Indya started to cry, and it became nearly impossible to pacify her with the backdrop of thunderstorms. Abhi was scared, too. He was unable to comprehend what was going around him. All of them got drenched in the rain.

Kabir realised that they were only a few streets away from Ibhrahim's house and stumbled upon a wooden fence meant to protect the cattle. Without anybody noticing them, he jumped over the fence, and helped Bhavi climb over it and snuck into the place.

It was a small farm with a few goats, some hens, and a cow. The animals had secured a position under the roof in one corner. The farm had a huge haystack on one side, and a long narrow water stream running in the middle. It was almost overflowing with rainwater, and an iron cage had a mother hen on the other side.

The goats and the cow were tied to a wooden post under the roof with a large rope. In the other corner of the farm, there was a pit filled with muck and animal waste. The entirety of the farm was filled with an overwhelming stench.

The owner of the farm probably lived in the house that was next to the farm. Kabir looked around on all sides, but there was no sign of any habitat inside it. He even went near the house and checked for people inside, but nobody answered. He decided to spend the daytime there and start at night.

Since they had been awake all through the night, Bhavi was extremely tired. She patted the kids dry and removed the wet clothes that were on them. Kabir arranged a pallet for Bhavi and spread the blanket that he had brought. He even tied the sling that they had made for Indya above the pallet onto the two posts, making it like a hammock, and placed Indya inside it. Kabir, Bhavi, and Abhi lay below the cradle, and he began to gently rock it.

Abhi and Indya fell asleep as the rain stopped gradually. The sun slowly came out, pushing the clouds aside.

Kabir said to Bhavi, 'You need to rest for a while. It's going to be a long journey tonight. We need to walk throughout the night to get to Kartarpur on time.'

Bhavi nodded. 'Okay… You, too, must get some sleep, then.'

I don't think I can sleep today. That sight of Daya and Laxmi lying there dead has destroyed me. This time, yesterday, we were loading our bags on Daya's cart. He was with us until yesterday. What wrong had he done in all his life? He was a good son, an obedient student, a caring husband, an excellent father, and above all, he was an amazing friend. How could Ibhrahim do this to us in the name of religion? My mind is going insane. I don't know whether to mourn for Daya's loss or Ibhu's betrayal. They both hurt me equally.'

Bhavi just looked at him and remained silent.

Kabir continued, 'He would not even bear the slightest of the pain. Even with empty pockets, he had the biggest smile on his face all day. He would do anything if it was for me and Ibhrahim.'

'I don't have any words to console you,' said Bhavi. 'Even if I did, I don't think it is possible to. Some people just come into our lives and our life can never be the same without them again. You had a million good memories with him. Just cherish them. I understand it's a huge loss and this is not the right way for death to embrace both Daya and Laxmi. Still, instead of mourning their loss, be glad for those years that you had to spend with him. We will bring up Abhi as Daya wanted him to be.'

'And Ibhrahim? I still can't believe he would go to this extent. What had these people done to Ibhu?'

'I understand. People are going crazy these days in the name of religion. What has happened has happened, and we should get over this. You know we are not safe here. What would have happened if you hadn't come to the attic? Or if Kaala hadn't given me the signal at the right time? But look... here we are. We don't know if we will even be able to cross the border alive. Maybe we should have stayed back in Rawalpindi. We don't know, Kabir. Three days before, they killed my father. Yesterday, it was Daya and Laxmi. Don't you see what is going on around us? We need to reach India. This doesn't feel like home anymore to me.'

Both of them heard interrupted voices from a radio.

They realised it was coming from the house adjacent to the wall on the rear-end of the farm. They could hear it, but it was disrupted and not clear. Kabir got up and followed the voice from the radio till where it could be heard clearly.

At the corner of the farm, he was able to hear the news. He tried to eavesdrop on the news from the radio. *'Murder and arson reach a new peak. Killings continue in the Indian-Punjab province 122 killed and 174 injured in the riots that happened yesterday.'*

Kabir suddenly remembered that his father was in Firozpur in the Indian-Punjab province. He believed that if he reached Kartarpur by 22nd, he could reach Firozpur by 23rd.However, three days were left for that, and the violence seemed to be escalating exponentially.

'Fires blaze all day long. Two places of worship were burnt down,' was what he heard from the radio again. And then, two people murmuring, *'This is the only thing on news these days. New killings and new blasts appear every day, everywhere.'*

Kabir did not make a sound and came back to Bhavi. He told her what he had heard.

'You must try contacting Abba once again and tell him that we are on our way,' suggested Bhavi. 'Also, ask him to be safe. He is all we have now.'

'I tried contacting his party office through the telephone line. Nobody responded. I wrote letters to him on August 15, conveying that Indya was born. But I am not sure any of those letters reached him.'

'Did you try checking the post office or the police station? They might know the means to contact on emergencies.'

'You are right,' said Kabir. 'I should at least let him know that we are on our way.'

'I can manage for a few hours. You go and check the post office or the police station in Sohawa. If they are open, then try to inform Abba and get help immediately. He might know how to get us out.'

August 20, 11 a.m.

Kabir adjusted the position of his *taqiyah* and noticed an umbrella hanging on the roof. He took that umbrella only to cover his face as much as possible. Before he left, Bhavi said, 'But make sure you return soon and be safe. Three of us are waiting here for you.'

Kabir smiled with pain and left the farm.

He asked the directions for the post office to people on the roads. There seemed to be less hustle that day in Sohawa, like the calmness restored after the storm. He reached the post office, only to see that it had been closed and sealed.

He inquired about it to the people nearby. Their reply was, 'It's been closed since the boundary line was announced. They don't want us to contact anybody.'

On the way back to the farm, he noticed a telephone booth, right at the centre of the bazaar, next to the police station. The shops in and around the bazaar were closed. He saw a few people gathered in front of the police station. He quickly went into the booth and dialled the number of his father's Indian National Congress party office at Firozpur.

It had already been an hour since he left the farm. He knew he must get back soon. To his surprise, he got the line, but nobody answered. As he dialled again, he saw a few members coming out of the police station through the glass doors of the booth, and one among them was Ibhrahim.

A ripple of outrage took form inside Kabir. They were just 100 metres apart. He immediately turned his head and hung the phone. He closed his eyes and remembered Bhavi's face. He needed to get to her.

He somehow picked up the feeling that Ibhrahim had seen him. He nonchalantly came out of the booth, opened his umbrella and started walking in the opposite direction. After a few minutes, he turned his head to check whether Ibhrahim was still there. As he turned, there he was. He was already looking at Kabir. Their eyes met for a fraction of a second.

Chapter Nine

THE ANIMAL FARM

August 20, 1 p.m.

Day 3

Kabir made his way back to the farm. Taking slow and steady steps, he kept thinking about his encounter with Ibhrahim. He had a strong gut feeling that he wouldn't chase him as he was just coming out of the police station after all. *Maybe, it was about Daya and Laxmi's death,* he thought.

Suddenly, he regretted not having performed their last funeral rites. 'Maybe what Bhavi said was right; right now, I don't know whether Bhavi and I will be able to cross the border alive. It's not for us. It is happening to thousands of people who try to leave the country,' he said to himself.

While the rest of the country was breathing the long-awaited freedom that they had wanted, in Punjab and Bengal, people were running for their lives. India's independence gave nothing to celebrate for them.

It was merely an announcement; an announcement that would

64

displace them for the rest of their lives. All those thoughts were fluttering inside his mind. He found a newspaper dated August 17, 1947, lying in front of a closed office building. He picked it up.

There were headlines about the announcement of the Radcliffe's line. 'A single man who had never been to India before decides on how to split India in 5 weeks. The line announced after independence only to avoid the blame falling on the British.' He crushed the paper and threw it away in anger. *After all these years of ruling us, you would have at least given us the freedom in a good way. You took more than 100 years to finally come to the decision of leaving us, but just 5 weeks on dividing us?* He thought.

He looked around for any shops to get something to eat for Bhavi and Abhi. All the shops were either sealed or burnt. Even the houses were shut. He knew he was still in Sohawa. The people who killed Daya and Laxmi would be still roaming there. So, he decided to get back to the farm, and leave Sohawa as soon as possible.

When he entered the farm, both Abhi and Bhavi were awake. Abhi was already starving. Kabir couldn't get him anything to eat. He didn't know anybody other than Ibhrahim in Sohawa.

Bhavi fed Indya, and the three of them only got to drink the rainwater that was collected in a pan in the early morning. Kabir didn't reveal about his encounter with Ibhrahim to Bhavi to avoid panic. He checked the hen's cage for any eggs. There was nothing. Somebody had already collected all the eggs. This made him realise that the owners might come in the evening to milk the cow.

Slowly, dusk fell. As they were planning to leave, an old man entered the farm. He was the owner of the farm, and he had been out all day. He was wearing a rusty brown kurta, white dhoti, and had a long, grizzled beard and a moustache. He walked towards the farm with an old woman by his side and stood speechless on seeing Abhi and the baby.

He scanned his entire farm with his bleary eyes. Everything

remained as he had left. They didn't seem robbers or rioters to him. 'All of you look like refugees. This is not an asylum. What are you doing inside my farm?' he yelled.

Kabir told him what had happened that made them take shelter here for the day and also said that they would leave the place as soon as the sun sets. But he remained non-committal about where he was headed. After what happened with Ibrahim, he couldn't afford to trust any other person. Religion drew even the sanest people mad.

The old man was Mohammad Haji who was a farmer in Sohawa. He and his wife, Fathima Moin, were residing here. They had a local shop that sold dairy products. Weeks before partition, his shop had been demolished in a clash between the Hindus and the Muslims. Many of his cows and goats were stolen during the unrest, because of which, they went into a huge debt and had no option but to sell their house. After having vacated all of their belongings, they just came to take whatever was left behind in the farm.

The sight of Bhavi holding a new-born softened Fathima's heart. She went near her and asked Bhavi, 'How old is the baby?'

'Five days,' Bhavi replied. Fathima took the baby in her arms. She was a compassionate woman. She looked at the baby, then at the mother.

'You look terrible, have you had anything to eat?' she asked.

'We had dinner last night,' Bhavi mellowed.

'You can't let yourselves starve like this. The baby needs you. You need to eat for the baby,' Fathima said and looked at Haji.

They had nothing to give them other than the cow. He sat down, cleaned the udder, and began to milk the cow. After minutes of pulling the teats, they finally collected enough milk. Fathima quickly heated up the milk in her backyard and gave it to Bhavi and Abhi, and Kabir drank whatever was left. It could not fill the tummy, but it did quench their thirst.

When they were about to leave, Haji looked at Indya, and said, 'It's okay that you don't want to reveal where you are going, but don't head towards the west. It's brimming with communal violence and be safe wherever you go.'

Kabir couldn't hold it within himself for long. He felt deep down that Haji could be trusted. He told him that they were headed for Kartarpur. That is when they came to know that Haji was selling his animals at Fatehpur which was on the way to Kartarpur. He readily offered a place for them in his cart.

Kabir saw Bhavi. She didn't give an answer.

'Not all of us are murderers. You can trust us,' Fathima broke the silence with those words.

August 20, 7 p.m.

An hour had passed since they had started their journey. Haji and Fathima were sitting on the front, with two massive bullocks pulling the cart, and Kabir with his family stayed on the back of the cart with four goats and a hen inside a cage. They had literally cramped themselves amidst them.

The cow was tied to the cart outside, and it kept following them. A few hours pass by, and a gush of darkness enshrouded them with the mooing and bleating of cattle in the background. They had to take the lesser-known road to avoid the crowds of migrants. It was an unpaved road with almost no lightings.

Bhavi had fallen asleep on Kabir's shoulders, conveniently wrapping her arms around his. Abhi reminded he was hungry again, and Kabir somehow kept on pacifying him. With every bump on the road, the old cart joggled. Bhavi clasped her belly and kept waking up. Her breasts were tender and swollen. The journey of all was very difficult for the new mother.

Kabir, feeling helpless, looked above. The sky was empty, there

were no stars, and it was a no moon day. He closed his eyes and sent forth a prayer and wondered what destiny had in store for them. As he did so, he easily felt the burning sensation in his eyes. It had been 2 days since he had slept. He dozed off in spite of him being wary of their journey.

At 9 p.m.

The cart halted as a group of militants suddenly appeared out of nowhere in the middle of the forest. They were stopped, and the militants checked Haji first. Kabir heard a few exchanges that took place between them.

The militants came to the back side of the cart and one among them flashed a torch light on Bhavi's face. She quickly turned away her face, adjusted her hijab covering her forehead. Those men were Muslims and Haji explained to them that they were relocating within Pakistan.

Bhavi still disguised as a Muslim woman, escaped their eyes. Another one enquired about their baggage. Kabir struggled to keep his expression neutral. He replied that they had lost everything on their way to a group of Hindus who charged at them. It seemed that their explanation sounded convincing for them that they decided to leave them. They took two of Haji's goats and left the place. Haji had no option but to forego them for Kabir's sake. The cart slowly started moving again.

At 11 p.m.

With a sudden bump, the back wheel got bogged into a mud pit on one side of the road. The cart failed to move in spite of Haji's maximum effort. He got down the cart and started pushing it from the back. Kabir tried to lift the wheel out with the best of his strength but was still unable to make a difference.

They brought all their animals out of the cart and tried pushing the cart again. All their efforts went in vain. They were stranded for an hour not knowing what to do. Eventually, Kabir realised that they had only one day to reach Kartarpur, and they must keep moving somehow.

So, he decided to walk on foot and did not waste a minute. He hugged Haji and said, 'We will forever be grateful for your help.' Haji smiled. 'This is just a small help that I could do for my fellow men. Don't worry. I hope you reach India safely.'

'You knew we were headed to India?' asked Bhavi with surprise.

'I found out that you have disguised the minute I saw you. What else could have made you hide in my farm, that, too, in a Muslim-majority-Sohawa?' Haji and Moin blessed Abhi and their baby. 'Barakallahu feek.'

Then, they parted ways.

Kabir, along with Abhi and Bhavi, carried Indya and began their arduous journey on foot. Wild bushes and shrubs surrounded either side of the road. There were hardly any lights on the road. But they could see lights at a distance which indicated that they were only a few kilometres away from Fatehpur.

Their plan was to keep walking till the sun rose, and then, to take rest wherever they found a place, as long as they kept moving. Kartarpur was more than 150 kilometres away from Fatehpur.

They reached Fatehpur in an hour and continued to walk towards the east. Bhavi got exhausted as her back began to ache. All she needed right at that time was rest. She badly needed to give her body the time and care that a new mother deserved. She struggled yet continued to walk. Kabir, on seeing this, got Indya from her, and let Abhi walk by himself.

August 21, 3 a.m.

Shabazpur

It'd been three hours since they had begun walking. They had a few stops on the way. The three of them were famished. They were weak, worn out, and hungry. As they reached the banks of the river Chenab, Bhavi suddenly slipped while placing her foot on the stones below, and her ankle got twisted.

After all that she had been through, it worsened her condition further. It hurt her like hell. She couldn't move an inch. Kabir was already carrying Indya in one hand but still lifted her. Abhi even made his contribution to help her stand with his tiny hands. Although she tried hard to supress her tears, it was evident that she needed rest.

They took a look around them. On the banks of the river, there were a few houses. They continued to walk towards them.

Bhavi was limping heavily, yet somehow managed to move with the twisted ankle little by little and moved near one of the houses. A sudden sharp excruciating pain went through her. She had stepped on an iron spike that had been lying around. She firmly kept her foot to the ground again. It pierced deep through her skin, making it enter a few more centimetres inside her foot. She fell back and sat. Kabir gave Indya to Bhavi, carefully lifted her foot, and slowly jiggled the iron spike out. Abhi was watching this scene, clueless, not knowing what to do.

Chapter Ten

BANANAS

August 21, 3:30 a.m.

Shabazpur

A gush of fresh blood came out through the cut. Kabir checked the iron spike; it wasn't rusted. He lifted Bhavi along with Indya and took her near the houses. Abhi came, following them, holding Kabir's kurta with his fingers.

They searched for people nearby, but all the houses seemed to be abandoned. Nobody lived there. Kabir decided to rest at one of these houses for a while. He entered a house; the doors were already left ajar. He took Bhavi inside. The house had a few pieces of furniture here and there. The shelves were empty. 'Whoever lived here must have left the house in a hurry,' Kabir said as he made Bhavi sit at a corner.

He examined the wound; it was kind of deep. Her ankle had already been twisted, and now, she had got a cut. He searched the house and found a small pot. He brought some freshwater from the river, cleaned her wound, and wrapped a towel around her wound

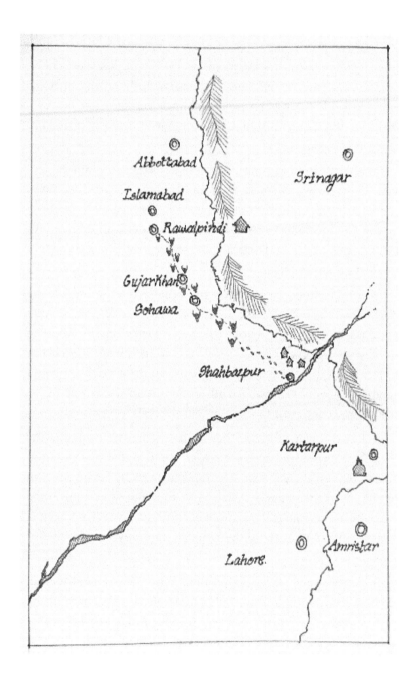

tightly. Her voice cracked when she tried to speak.

Kabir went near her. Her face, once radiant, had lost all its radiance and charm. It was painful to see her in that state. All he could do was embrace her and let the torrent of her tears soak his shirt. He could hear her suffocating with each breath, her eyes screaming out its pain. Abhi sat by her side and slowly patted her ankle with his hands.

It had been an hour. Indya began to cry. Abhi was hungry, too. Even Bhavna was extremely tired and hungry. She said to Kabir, 'You must get anything for us to eat. Leave crossing the border alive, we won't be even able to make it near the border without food. All of us are starving Kabir. Look at Abhi. I have to feed Indya also. We can't leave them like this.'

Kabir understood the situation and wondered what he could do. He searched the entire house for any leftover eatables. Not a grain of rice was to be found. He opened the wooden almirahs mounted on the walls and found a torch. He adjusted its rim and switched it on. It seemed to be functioning. He checked the shelves again and found some coins. He grabbed all of them, loaded them up in his pockets, and continued to search under the bed.

He found a pair of old leather sandals. One was torn, and the other one was in a wearable condition. He took that one with him and put that on Bhavi's foot. The sandals probably belonged to an old man. It was way bigger than Bhavi's foot. But now, it just fitted her right as her ankle had swollen and was layered up with a bandage. Other than those, he couldn't find anything useful for them.

He came out and searched the other house. They were all locked. He tried to break in, but he couldn't. Helplessly, he looked at the ghastly rapid river flowing in front of him. A much darker reality weaved through his mind. *Even the river is flowing in the direction opposite to India,* he thought.

At that moment, for the first time, he wondered whether all these efforts were going to be fruitful. Taking Indya to India became a distant dream. He closed his eyes and could hear the stream gurgling and the water splashing against all the boulders on its way. He remembered his father's words, 'You should never let your life stagnate; you should keep moving however bad the situations are.' It gave him a new hope.

He opened his eyes, bent down to scoop a handful of water, and drank it. It was thirst-quenching. The words "never stagnate and keep moving" repeated on his mind as he splashed some water on his face and found a banana leaf floating on the water, reaching his side of the bank. It was coming from the other side of the river. He woke up and realised there might be a banana farm on that side of the river.

He went inside the house and informed Bhavi about that. She asked him to take Abhi with him to get some bananas as quick as possible. 'I can manage until then,' Bhavi assured him.

Yet, Kabir was not convinced, and he was not ready to leave her alone in an unknown place.

Bhavi said, 'Look, Kabir, there is no one here and the people who lived here had abandoned their houses and left. Nobody is going to come here in the first place. You must go and get something for us to eat.'

Kabir sighed. 'Okay. I will get something. But remember, whatever happens, we need to be at Kartarpur on August 22nd at 2 p.m. That is our only safe chance of crossing the border.'

'I know. But starving like this, we can't even walk anymore. I have a baby to feed and there is Abhi. We need to eat something.'

Kabir lifted Abhi and ran his fingers through his hair. 'We are going to find some fruits and bring you. Okay, Abhi?' he said to him. He agreed and rested his head on Kabir's shoulders. A three-year-old couldn't react more than this. He had already been missing his parents, and though he could not put it into words, it was evident from his face.

'Just one more day, and we will be in India,' Kabir said to Bhavi and smiled.

Bhavi, noticing the small dimples on his cheek, smiled back, and responded, 'But be safe.'

He took a small dagger from their bag and left the house with Abhi. After walking a certain distance along the bank, he found a wooden bridge to the other side of the bank. It was old and had wooden logs arranged one after the other with small irregular gaps in between. He cautiously stepped onto the bridge checking its stability.

It gave the impression of having worn out from long use, but still fulfilled its purpose. It was anchored well on his side. He slowly stepped onto the deck and placed his leg, holding Abhi in one hand and clutching the handrail of the bridge with another. The little one was terrified as Kabir kept walking with his hand becoming tighter with every step. 'Abhi, close your eyes. Don't open them unless I tell you to,' Kabir said to him as he shut his eyelids.

Kabir could feel the vigour of the river current. He knew that even one wrong step would put them in great danger. When he was halfway through, he turned back and looked at the houses. There were 10 to 15 of them, but he made sure that he could identify the house where Bhavi and Indya were. He took a deep breath and continued to walk again.

He reached the end of the bridge. In front of him, there were only wild shrubs and bushes. There was no sight of a banana farm. He kept walking along the bank for a while, and after some time, he reached a fence made up of vertical bars of stones and iron cables knotted in between, inside which he found a banana plantation.

He jumped the fence easily and entered inside. The sweet aroma

of bananas made its way into his nostrils. They were arranged in
rows.

Kabir placed his foot on the moist soil below. His entire foot got
buried in the soil. He switched Abhi to his other arm since it had
started aching from carrying him for a long time. He took the dagger
out and started cutting some bananas. He placed them on a banana
leaf and wrapped them tightly. He loaded as many bananas as he
could.

There was a cacophony of animal calls in the background. He
packed the bananas as quick as possible as he suddenly heard a few
voices coming from behind. He turned back to scan the area under
the light of a lamp post at one corner of the farm, where he saw a
group of around 10 to 15 men sitting in a semi-circle with a man
standing in the middle.

Fire was lit beside them. All of them seemed to be wearing a
taqiyah, confirming their identity. Kabir, without making a noise,
hushed Abhi to be quiet. He slowly took the banana package and
hastened to leave. As he took his first foot out of the wet soil, he
heard 'Kartarpur...' Yeah! He heard that right. They were
murmuring something about Kartarpur. He stopped to rethink what
he had just heard. He hid behind the bushes and tried to listen to
what they were discussing.

'Those mongrels are thinking that we don't know about their
plan to enter India through Kartarpur,' a man was saying.

'We must teach a lesson to everyone who is trying to leave our
Pakistan,' said another.

'It's a chance of a lifetime to hunt all of them together in one
place.'

'But Kartarpur is filled with Sikhs on both the sides. It's not going
to be easy to tackle them. They will try their best to let the Hindus
pass the border,' a fourth voice said.

'Yeah, that's right, and that is why we will hit the Sikhs first. We will hit them so hard that they can hardly get up.'

'That sounds like a convincing plan. We need to gather more of our men.'

'But isn't Kartarpur a holy place for Sikhs? How can we execute our plan in a holy place? Isn't it a grave sin for us?'

'We are not sinning. We are doing a religious cleansing.'

A pack of stray dogs howled at the top of their voice behind Kabir.

The group of men turned around and looked out for the noise. Kabir realised that he couldn't stay there any longer and decided to make his way out of the farmyard. He carefully placed his step, making sure to avoid the joggling of the coins on his pocket. While he was about to jump off the fence, he saw the pack of dogs fighting over each other. He got hold of the stones that he found lying near him and threw them at the dogs. They growled and left the place.

Kabir peeled off a banana and gave one to Abhi. It was a few minutes after he had started walking along the banks of the river that he saw fire blazing at a distance. It took him a moment to comprehend that those were the houses he had left Bhavi and Indya.

'Bhavi!' he yelled and ran toward the bridge. On one hand, he had Abhi, and on the other hand was holding the bananas that he had packed. He held the handrail of the bridge, and time was ticking. With every passing second, the fear inside him grew. He forgot the current of the river. The gaps in between those broken logs didn't bother him anymore. And as he ran, the leaf gave away and a few bananas fell to the ground.

He identified the house Bhavi and Indya were staying in. It was blazing with flames on all sides. He tried to enter the house, but the doorway had collapsed, preventing him from entering. He went to the side of the house and looked inside through the window. Bhavi

and Indya were not there. There wasn't a single trace of them; even their bag was not there.

Chapter Eleven

THE RESCUE

August 21

Shabazpur

A few hours ago

Bhavi looked out from a window and saw Kabir getting tinier as he moved away from the house. She let out a deep sigh, looked at her ankle, and tried to move it. She could move it, but it wasn't easy for her. She fed Indya and put her to sleep.

She looked at the empty and pitch-black sky. She tried to fall asleep, but the pain kept haunting her. She knew she had to get some rest. She closed her eyes, and the first thing that flashed in front of her eyes was Kabir's face.

The very thought of it brought a smile to her face. She kept visualising the tension lines on his forehead, his arch-like eyebrows that almost met at the centre, his black iris like the night sky without a single cloud but with a tint of brownish hue, and the dimple on his cheeks that formed when he smiled. There was nothing greater than his face that could bring contentment and calmness inside her. She slowly began to doze off.

After a while, she woke up on hearing a crowd approaching and looked out to find a few raucous youths shouting slogans, setting the abandoned houses on fire. They threw kerosene over the roof-top and tossed off a burning log on it. Not knowing what to do, she tried to get up and stand on her feet. It hurt like never before. With great difficulty, she balanced herself, took her bag, and left the house before they approached her.

With every step, her pain intensified. She had to fight with all her might. Tightening the sandal, she continued to walk. She put in all her strength and took Indya outside that arena. After coming to a certain distance, unable to keep another foot, she sat down, hiding herself under a boulder at the bank of the river.

She removed her footwear and looked at her foot. The towel had soaked in blood. She cried in vain. She could feel the sound of her heartbeat as the turmoil inside her took another form. It was in situations like these that she wondered whether God really existed. She turned back to see whether they had left, but they hadn't.

They were still coming further on her way. She looked at Indya like the last scintillation in the darkness surrounding her. She got up and walked again, placing her step faster this time. She proved her mettle, and in a few minutes, she got to a road that was divided into two. Not knowing which one to take, she stood at the middle of the road and got a slight feeling of light-headedness. She sweated instantaneously, and the last thing she saw before blacking out was a bullock cart approaching her.

When she woke up, she was on the side of the road with an elderly woman splashing some water on her face, giving her a few sips of water to drink. She could hear another young lady pacifying Indya as she cried at the top of her voice.

Jan 25, 2021

New Delhi

Decades passed, and Indya was still crying. Tears finally found their way to her eyes after days of being dry.

Jothi interrupted saying, 'Ma… your dinner is ready.'

Indya wiped her tears as Jothi came with the food near her.

'Ma… I have made your favourite mushroom soup with a little cream; just how you would like it.'

There was still no response from Indya.

Jothi had been taking care of Indya for the past seven years and was more like a family member now. She was hired by her son, Amir, to take care of Indya. Jothi cooked her favourite meal, washed her clothes, took care of the house, and made sure that she had her medicines and food on time.

Time had taken a severe toll on Indya, both physically and mentally. Her fingers were inflamed from the cold, her voice had become feeble, her spine had lost its curvature, her knees were no more able to make her stand upright, her hands were always shaky, and her vision was blurry, but she had this clear memory of the events that unfolded during her childhood. The stories her mother had told her back then. Her memory was the only thing she was holding onto, in addition to the life inside her.

She slowly slurped the soup in front of her in a bowl and could taste the creaminess. Yes, it was creamy and just the way she liked. She looked at Jothi who was standing nearby and gave her a smile.

Jothi smiled back, and now, she knew that the soup was truly delicious. She went inside and came back with the medicines as Indya had finished her soup.

After taking the medicines, she asked Jothi to put her to bed, and continued the book exactly from where she had left.

August 21, 1947

5 a.m.

Slowly, Bhavi woke up and realised that she had fainted. In the fog of her waking mind, she asked the lady, 'Is my baby okay? Did anything hurt her?'

'Your baby is completely fine,' answered the young lady.

Bhavi looked around her and found a Sikh family. There was a man named Sardar Ajeet Singh. In his late fifties, he looked tall and well-built with a turban on his head and a rifle hanging on his shoulders. His wife, Poonam, and his three daughters, Srimayee, Aashu, and Soni were fleeing from Fatehpur.

'What happened to you? What are you doing here at this time all alone?' asked Aashu.

Bhavi sobbed, 'They have killed my father and my friends. My husband and I escaped with the baby.'

Srimayee asked, 'Where is your husband?'

Bhavi was unable to speak as she choked on her tears.

'But you look like a Muslim,' said Aashu. 'Why did you have to escape?'

Bhavi took out the Mangalsutra (the sacred necklace worn by Hindu women as symbol of being married) that she had been hiding all that time and showed it to them. 'I'm not a Muslim. I had no other way.'

'Enough of your questions. The poor girl is exhausted. Give her something to eat,' said Poonam sternly.

Soni took out a bottle of sherbet and gave it to Bhavi. She drank all of it in one go.

Ajeet said to her, 'See, *beta* (dear child), we can't stay here for long. It's not safe. We are going to Kartarpur. Do you want to come with us? It's safe there.'

Bhavi looked back and wondered whether she should wait there for Kabir or go with this family to Kartarpur. She didn't know when Kabir might come. It'd been hours and she knew she could not wait here in this way with the baby. She remembered what Kabir had said. 'Whatever happens, we should be in Kartarpur on 22nd at 2 p.m.'

Soni got the baby from Bhavi and helped her climb onto their cart. They started moving. Srimayee noticed her ankle was bleeding. She removed the towel to check the wound. 'It's deep. You should not walk with this leg anymore. It needs some rest,' she said. She, then, asked for the bottle of kerosene that Ajeet had packed with them. Ajeet gave her the bottle and she poured some of it on her wound, cleaned it with a cloth and wrapped it back again tightly.

'Why are you going to Kartarpur?' Bhavi asked Poonam.

'Our ancestors have been living in Fatehpur for more than 100 years. My husband owns a rice grain shop, and these are my three daughters. When the news about the partition came, we were worried on which side we would fall. But our neighbours, who were Muslims mostly, promised to take care of us even if Fatehpur went to Pakistan. We have been coexisting in harmony for ages. We exchanged sweets and celebrated functions together. We shared a mutual respect and lived happily until the news about partition wavered. When the lines were announced, the neighbours who had promised to protect us were the first ones to attack us. Last night, not knowing what to do, we sealed all our doors and windows and remained inside the house. They came late at night, shouting at our doors to open them. I remember seeing through the keyhole. They were 4 in number with daggers and rods on their hands. Ajeet lost his patience and even got his rifle ready. We almost thought of killing our daughters since it was a better way to die than getting caught in those hands. We know what happened to the Sikh women from our village. They poured kerosene and set themselves on fire. Ajeet was on the verge of shooting his own daughters. That is when they finally broke the door and Ajeet, in a reflex, started firing. He shot two of them. The bullet went through one man's jaw and came out through the back of his skull. The next bullet went through another man's abdomen, tearing his organs apart. Both of them fell on the ground and died. On seeing this, the other two fled. They went to bring in more help. We decided not to stay here for long and took what all we could and left the home without telling anybody at the stroke of midnight.'

The pain and frustration behind her eyes were evident from her voice.

'We chose this route in spite of knowing it's unpaved and takes more time, because it was lesser known,' added Ajeet.

'We had even set our Srimayee up for marriage. They were to get married in two months. But now, we don't even know if he is even alive,' said Poonam.

Bhavi replied, 'Look what this partition has done to us. A country, like an ancestral property, is getting divided amongst brothers.'

Bhavi told them the story about her journey from Rawalpindi, the things that happened at Sohawa, and what had happened to Daya and Laxmi, and why Kabir left them in Shabazpur.

Ajeet said, shaking his head, 'I can't believe people have become this irrational and turned barbaric.'

'Does Kabir know that you are headed to Kartarpur?' Aashu asked Bhavi.

Bhavi nodded. 'He will know, and he will be there tomorrow, but how come you are sure that Kartarpur will be a safe place?'

'It's neither a Muslim nor a Hindu majority area. It's full of Sikhs. We know our people. Outsiders cannot enter Kartarpur easily,' responded Ajeet.

Bhavi said mournfully, 'No place can be trusted as long as it lies on this side of the partition line.'

Ajeet heard her but did not utter a word. It got him thinking.

What she said just now was true. He knew it in his heart that it was true.

Exhausted by the day's events, Bhavi closed her eyes, giving them the rest they needed, as Ajeet kept riding the cart.

Kabir was not beside her, but she was not alone this time. Bhavi had every hope that Kabir would make it to Kartarpur the next day.

August 21, 11 a.m.

The sun was right above. Ajeet needed to give the bullocks some rest. He stopped the cart for a while under a Peepal tree. Everyone got down the cart. Indya was still asleep in Soni's arms. Aashu helped Bhavi get down. She was not placing her thorn-pricked leg down. She hopped on with her another leg.

All of them sat down under the shade of the tree and began to have their breakfast that they had brought from home—a few apples, carrots, some roti, and some home-made mango pickle. They shared it among themselves and saved the remaining to eat later that day. They had packed a few items to eat for not less than three to four days. They expected the worst but were not sure how long the journey might take.

Bhavi kept thinking about Kabir—whether he had had his food, whether he had guessed that she would be going to Kartarpur, about Abhi, whether he missed his parents and whether he was alright.

She ate the fruits somehow and saw the family in front of her, chatting with one another, and how Ajeet took care of his daughters. It reminded her of her father. *How would things have been if he were here now?* She thought to herself. Fresh tears welled in her eyes and sadness mounted her as she recollected her moments with her father. She found it difficult to swallow the roti. It felt as if it had got stuck in the middle of her food pipe.

The family noticed that she was not alright. Ajeet promised her, 'Everything will be alright. Acceptance is the key. You just need some courage right now to fight the reality.' His demeanour exuded warmth, just like her father.

Chapter Twelve

THE LAST LAP OF THE JOURNEY

August 21, 1947

8 p.m.

On the way to Kartarpur

The cart halted as it got stuck amidst a crowd in the middle of the way. Thousands of people had gathered to protest the partition. They protested with slogans and wouldn't accept the Radcliffe's boundary line. They wanted it to be reconsidered. 'What's the point in fighting now? It's too late for anything to be changed,' said Ajeet in a furious tone.

As time went by, the mob increased in numbers slowly. Soon, there were clashes among the crowd where they began pelting stones against each other. Ajeet and his family, along with Bhavi, hardly had any clue how to escape.

He slowly turned his cart and started moving back in the direction they had come from. They were left with the only option of taking another route, which was the longer one indeed. If they had proceeded at the same pace on that route, they would have

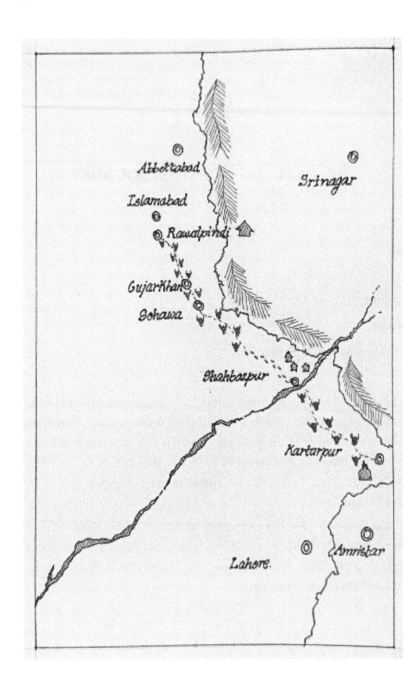

reached Kartarpur before the sun rose. However, it was going to be noon even if they had travelled without any breaks.

This path was also not as clear as they had expected. Many people had turned back as the road had been blocked by the protesters. Most of them were on foot with some baggage on their heads and the rest tied to their shoulders. The carts were heavily loaded with people. There were so many people on one cart that the bullocks found it so hard to pull them.

August 22, 1947

The sky slowly lightened. Bhavi opened her eyes. It was not just another regular day. It was the day they had been waiting for. All their hopes dangling in the thread of Kartarpur, Ajeet made the cart move a little faster. The only thing on his mind was that they were to be at Kartarpur as soon as possible.

The sun was at its zenith. They were only a few kilometres away from Kartarpur. Ajeet had spread a shawl above them and tied it to the corners of the cart just to safeguard the women and the baby from the scorching sun. Bhavi was thinking of all the ways to find Kabir. She decided to wait inside the Gurdwara at the heart of Kartarpur, hoping Kabir would come looking for her. Little did she know that Kabir would never go inside Kartarpur.

Half an hour passed, and they arrived at an arch with two pillars on either side of the road with the sign "Welcome to Kartarpur". Ajeet saw the sign, but Bhavi failed to notice that as she was hiding under the cover that was above her. Kabir was right there beside one of the pillars, waiting for Bhavi with Abhi.

He failed to notice the cart and kept searching for her among the people who came by walk. Ajeet noticed the young man with a boy in one hand, restless and searching for someone. The cart slowly moved past Kabir, and suddenly, he heard someone yelling at the top of his voice, 'Bhavi!'

Ajeet stopped his cart, and he could hear it for the second time. 'Bhavi!' It was the young man who stood beside the entry pillar. Bhavi heard that call and immediately shouted back, 'Kabir!' The moment he heard her voice, he came running to the cart and helped her get down. They hugged each other, and the group experienced a momentary surge of happiness.

Tears saturated her eyes, spilling out. He put her hijab back in position and kissed her forehead. He took Indya onto his arms and said, 'I'm never ever going to leave you both alone hereafter.'

At 1 p.m.

Kabir tried convincing Ajeet and his family to the best of his ability, but it was of no use. In spite of him narrating them what he had heard yesterday from a group of militants, Ajeet still believed that Kartarpur was the safest place for them. So, Kabir and Bhavi decided to leave Kartarpur, half hearted.

She spent a few more minutes with them, and Kabir gestured Bhavi that it was time to leave. She had hardly spent a day with this family, but it felt as if they had known each other for years. Bhavi longed to thank them but stood speechless, not knowing the right words to speak.

She fell on the feet of Ajeet and Poonam to get their blessings, and they bade the family farewell. Bhavi wondered whether she would be able to see them again. 'They were good people, Kabir,' she said to him as their cart slowly entered the Kartarpur territory.

'Maybe, what I heard was just a plan that never gets executed,' Kabir replied in a calm tone.

'I really wish it was just a plan,' Bhavi replied, and they slowly made their way to a nearby railway station, only to find that it was flooded with people. Kabir decided to board the next train that came their way.

They enquired the station master about the train service. They were told that the next train to Lahore was at 2 p.m. Bhavi's condition was not good. Crossing the border right now amidst all the chaos was much more daunting than they had imagined. It'd been five days since they had left Rawalpindi.

During this journey, Bhavi had already lost her father, Kabir had seen his dearest friend getting murdered cruelly and another one betraying him in the name of religion. Kabir realised that both of them had literally escaped from the verge of death, had been running for their lives and for food for the past few days. After this vicious circle, yet they still continued on this journey with the only hope of crossing the border and entering India via Kartarpur on August 22. However, now they were moving away from the border. They were actually moving still further inside the heart of Pakistan.

They were so close, just a matter of few kilometres between the two countries and still, Kabir decided to move to Lahore. To him, right now, Bhavi was his first priority, and he was sick of running from place to place.

The four of them waited at the station, and Kabir checked Bhavi's leg. The bleeding had stopped, but the swelling didn't seem to be getting better. Kabir heard the sound of a train. He got up and stared at the train coming from a distance like a small brown box blowing out thick black smoke.

It made a screeching stop in front of him, and before it had even fully stopped, people started hopping onto it. He had the baby hanging on a sling on his torso along with a rope tied on Abhi's waist, and the end of the rope was tied to his hand. He made sure not to lose him in that crowd.

Bhavi stood beside him, clasping his arms more tightly than ever. As soon as the train stopped, he blocked the entrance and made Bhavi and Abhi move inside. People started pushing him aside and he somehow got inside luckily. The train was jam-packed in two minutes. Not an inch was left without people occupying.

Bhavi and Kabir lodged themselves in a confined space. Even when the train was ready to leave, people continued to climb its roof and the compartments overflowed. People hardly had any space to breathe. The train reeked of sweat, blood, and most of all, panic.

The train reached Lahore station by 9 p.m. A journey that would usually take 4 hours took almost 7 hours that day because of the people flooding the trains and the stations. Kabir was jostled by the passengers on a rush to get to the gates. In an attempt to move out of the train, someone stomped heavily on Bhavi's foot. Not able to keep another step, she got stuck in the crowd.

Kabir waited for everyone to leave, and then got down the train last with Bhavi. He got hold of her and landed at the Lahore station. He glanced at her foot. The cloth had been soaked in blood, and now, fresh blood was dripping from its edges. He made her sit in one corner of the station. Not knowing where to go, he thought of the last time he had come to Lahore. It was with his Abba, many years ago, to meet his friend who was then living a few streets away from the Lahore station. He decided to get his help and carefully took Bhavi to his house.

They reached the house only to find that it was locked. He asked the neighbours. Even they had no clue where he had gone. It was Zahir, Abba's dearest friend since childhood. He had met Kabir many a time. When Kabir lost his mother, he was the one who encouraged his father to join the British-Indian Army.

They waited outside his house till the midnight, and that was when a neighbour of his revealed that he had gone to his son's house in India. 'When will he be coming back?' asked Kabir.

The man replied, 'I don't think he will be ever coming back.'

Kabir finally decided to break the house open. They entered the

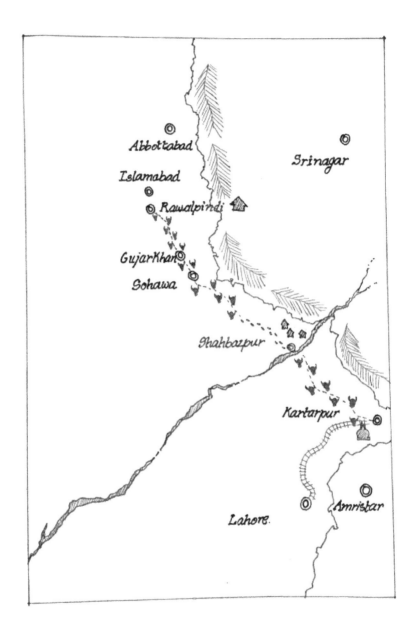

house without anybody noticing them. That night was meant to be spent there.

Chapter Thirteen

NEW BEGINNINGS

August 23, 1947

Lahore

The next morning, Kabir woke up early for his morning prayer. He had lost track of time and missed his prayers those days.

In the washroom, Kabir found a mirror. He looked at his face, noticing tired eyes sunken into their sockets, swollen eye bags, and the dark circles that had developed around his eyes. The past few days of exhaustion had taken a heavy toll on him. He took off the bandage that had been plastered on his forehead. He slowly pulled it away and found three sutures. The middle one had slightly given away. He cleaned the wound, took a bath, and wore Zahir's clothes which he had found inside the closet.

Bhavi had crashed into a deep sleep the previous night, and all she did the whole day was just sleep and catch up on all the rest that she had missed for the past few days. The only time she had woken up was to feed Indya and crashed again.

Abhi woke up at noon. Kabir managed to get a few supplies from the neighbours, and he prepared a vegetable soup with all that he had and gave it to Abhi. He made sure that the doors and the windows were sealed. His heart could not afford to lose one more beloved.

Kabir walked around the house, checking for anything that might be useful for them. He kept thinking whether it was right on his part to break open Zahir's house and staying in it without his knowledge. Nevertheless, due to thousands of people changing countries, the left-over houses were allocated to refugees. Kabir consoled himself with the fact that, anyhow, this house was going to be given to another Muslim family from India.

Kabir checked the bedroom. Bhavi was asleep. He sat next to her, watching her sleeping. She slowly opened her eyes, her heart still heavy from all that she had witnessed in the past few days. Yet, her eyes had signs of new hope. After all, it was Kabir's face that she was seeing as the first thing as she woke up. She looked at him, still half asleep, but a quick smile creased her face.

Her eyes were brimming with the desire to live in one place forever. Her smile was contagious. Kabir smiled back and admired her black flowing hair. He combed through her loose hair and continued doing so until she was wide awake. Bhavi asked for the time, quickly made a high bun with her hair, and tried to get up. The minute she landed her foot on the floor, she was screaming in pain. For a moment, she had forgotten about her foot.

Kabir checked the wound and realised she needed medical help. He slowly helped her balance with the other leg, and for the rest of the day, she needed Kabir to switch places.

Bhavi came out of the bathroom with wet hair, opened the window, the breeze drying her hair slowly, and she noticed how life was back on the streets of Lahore.

As the day progressed, her leg was getting worse. She had developed fever and her leg had swollen badly. She was experiencing such excruciating pain on her foot that she could no longer walk.

Kabir took her to a nearby hospital. The doctor cleaned her wound thoroughly, bandaged it, gave her some medicines, and recommended bed rest for at least two weeks as she was in the risk of developing sepsis.

Kabir now had no other option than to stay back at Lahore for another two weeks. On their way back home, they decided to stay in Lahore for some more time as that was the best available option in their hands.

As they were just about to enter the house, a voice from behind greeted them. It was Abdul, living in the adjacent house. Abdul was in his thirties, with a long beard and a warm smile. He had been Zahir's neighbour for quite a long time.

They exchanged a 'hello' and told him that they were Zahir's relatives from Baremullah (Kashmiri side of India) and were going to stay in his house for a few days. He welcomed them to Pakistan wholeheartedly and asked them to call him for any help without any hesitation. Kabir smiled back, waved a thank you, and entered the house.

'He seems to be nice,' said Bhavi.

'Yes... the first person to welcome us in Pakistan,' replied Kabir and slowly made Bhavi sit on the bed. Indya had become restless since the past few days and had been crying continuously. All their efforts to pacify her went in vain.

Kabir took Indya in his arms and kept walking inside the house, rhythmically patting her back gently. He noticed this sweet and pleasant milk smell coming from her. Her scent instantly released mountains of dopamine inside him and made him feel good.

Abhi, who was playing inside the house, found a radio in one corner of the hall. He switched it on. Nothing but flickering voices came from it. Kabir heard those voices and kept adjusting its frequency with a tiny bit of hope that he would be able to get some information on the status outside.

Finally, after adjusting the frequency for half an hour, Kabir could hear voices. 'Hindus and Sikhs were killed in a massacre at Kartarpur. Not even the new-borns were spared.' Bhavi happened to hear that.

She rushed forward to turn up its volume. 'With the Hindus from Pakistan planning to cross the border via Kartarpur escorted by Sikhs, their families were butchered even before the Hindus started arriving at Kartarpur. Women jumped into wells. They found drowning dignified than getting caught in the hands of the mobs. Some immolated themselves. Men killed their women to safeguard their honour. The remaining Sikhs ran to the Indian side for their lives. According to reports, the death toll may be as high as 1000. This turns out to be the worst mass communal clash, ever since the boundary line was announced.'

Kabir switched it off and took a few minutes to compose himself after hearing the news. He sat lifeless on a chair. Beside him was Bhavi, devastated by the mere thought of it. Their brains couldn't comprehend what they had just heard. If Kabir had not gone to the farm that day leaving Bhavi alone, he would not have heard the plan of the militants, and they could have easily been one among the thousands at the Kartarpur massacre.

'How could somebody commit such a heinous act? What are the governments and police doing?' seethed Bhavi.

'The Indian government is not responsible for what is happening on this side,' said Kabir.

'It seems like the decades of peaceful coexistence has suddenly become alien.'

Kabir remained quiet.

He never knew the situations would go to this extreme when he began his journey from Rawalpindi. The only thing that was on his mind then was, 'How am I ever going to cross the border?'

Bhavi thought of Ajeet's family. She prayed with all every last bit of hope left in her that they set foot in India somehow. Then, suddenly, a vivid thought took form inside her. Was it enough for just Ajeet's family to enter India? What about the hundreds of others who had tried? What about the thousands of others who were still trying to reach India? Whose fault was all this? All of a sudden, a line had made them alien in their own country. Was it their fault to fall on the other side of the line? Who was responsible for all this chaos and the tragedies that had unfolded since the announcement of the line?

People were trying to cross borders for survival to live, not die in the process of doing so. What was the whole point in crossing the border then? They could have lived in their old places than risk their lives and die trying to enter another country, she contemplated.

No amount of sleep could help her escape the memories of the atrocities that she had witnessed. That day slowly passed by, and the next day, Kabir woke up early as usual in the morning, and went for a walk on the streets. Most of the money that he had brought with him from Rawalpindi was left back in Ibhrahim's house while escaping. He was not sure of the number of days that he could survive with the meagre amount that was left with him.

The doctor had strictly instructed Bhavi to take rest for the next two weeks, making it impossible for them to continue their journey. He knew they needed some more money to cross the borders, but the only person they knew in Lahore was not there.

It had just dawned. Kabir stared at the empty street. As he kept walking, he stumbled upon a half-broken, burnt cycle-rickshaw near him. It was damaged, yet the inner frame was still intact.

Either the person who owned the rickshaw was not there anymore, or because of its condition, he would have left that on the road. That was when it struck him that he could put this rickshaw to some use. He slowly tried to move it, and the wheels came out of the mud with a screeching noise.

Zahir's house was only a few houses away. He carefully pulled the rickshaw and took it to his backyard. He started splashing water on the rickshaw. The black soot gave away, and he could clearly see the parts that had been damaged. He needed to change the frame of one of the wheels. He made a covering above, and he thought that if he painted the rickshaw, it would be done.

He sought the help of their neighbour Abdul and also bought the necessary materials from the nearby market. Abdul was kind enough to lend his tools and give Kabir a hand while repairing the rickshaw.

The two men started fixing the rickshaw around 9 in the morning, and it went on till sunset. It took Kabir two days to bring the rickshaw back in form. He painted the body of the rickshaw in bright yellow, and Bhavi did her magic by bringing in some more colours. They took some old blankets from Zahir's house and covered the seat. The wheels were changed, and oil was applied, so that it was smooth to pedal.

A day later, Kabir took the cycle-rickshaw and went to the railway station. As people were changing towns, the station was crowded as expected and flooded with people who badly needed a vehicle to carry their luggage and themselves.

His idea worked; people approached him as soon as they heard the noise that he made with his bell. He took people who wanted to travel short distances. Old people, disabled men and children hopped on his cycle. This went on for the whole day as he came back home exhausted in the evening. But he was happy that he could earn some money. Few days later, the officials from the newly formed Pakistan visited their house. They had come to enquire about the details of the people who had decided to stay back, that is, their new citizenship. Kabir gave them the details, telling them that they were a Muslim family. Kabir and Shabnam, who had come to Pakistan from Baremullah, Kashmir, with their three-year-old kid, Hussain, and their new-born daughter, Moin.

They were asked for their thumb imprints in the register and were asked for a few other miscellaneous details like their educational qualification, and about the rest of their family members.

When enquired about the property, he told them the house had belonged to his uncle Zahir who had left it for him and went to India during partition. The officials noted down everything and left the place.

Chapter Fourteen

THE JOB OFFER

September 10, 1947

A few weeks passed by. Bhavi's leg was getting better. She was now able to walk and do the chores on her own.

The next day, Kabir had gone out to run a few errands, and Bhavi was busy with the kids. Suddenly, she heard some strange voices outside her front door. First, a knock, then a pause, and several other knocks followed by it.

Bhavi moved towards the window to find three men standing outside their house. One among them was Abdul. She was doubtful at first, but then, she had to open the door since it was Abdul. She quickly adjusted the drape around her head and checked for the kids. They were inside the room.

Bhavi went to Abhi and told him, 'Do not come out of the room until I say so.' The happenings had made Abhi well aware of the situation, and he was able to grasp situations now. He looked at Bhavi as a mother after all those days of struggle. Abhi gave a nod as the thuds on the door began to pace up. She left the room to open the front door.

Abdul stood there without speaking a word. The other men explained that they were local officials from Lahore who had come to enquire if Bhavi was really from Baremullah. She recalled the officials had visited them last week and these guys had some other purpose.

As she stood wondering not knowing what to answer, Abdul told her not to panic that they were guys from the local office who just wanted to meet Kabir.

She explained that Kabir had gone out and also that they were from Baremullah. They threw a strange look, taking a glance at the interiors of the living room. They couldn't assess further as Bhavi was holding the door half-open. After asking Kabir to meet them at their office when he came back, they left.

Hundreds of questions arose in her mind. She imagined the worst possible things that could happen. 'Maybe it was nothing more than a procedural visit,' she said to herself, badly wanting to cling on to like it was the truth. But deep down, she knew something was not right.

After an hour, she couldn't hold herself and went to meet Abdul. When she knocked on his door, a young woman appeared. She had blue eyes with jet black kajal applied on her lower eyelids. She welcomed Bhavi inside with a smile.

'Hi. I'm Bha...' Bhavi began but corrected herself in time. 'I'm Shabnam. I'm staying in the next house. Is Abdul Bhaiyya (elder brother) at home?'

'*Haan*... Shabnam... Yes, yes. Come in... Have a seat.' Bhavi wondered who the lady was as she had never seen her there before.

The lady, who guessed what Bhavi was thinking about, opened up. 'I'm Nisma, Abdul's wife.'

'But I have never seen you here before.'

'During the partition, I had gone to my Papa's place. Now that things have settled, I have come back here,' Nisma explained.

'Oh… okay…'

'So, how are you related to Zahir Dada? Abdul told me you are his relatives.'

Bhavi took a minute and answered that Zahir Dada was Kabir's Dad's brother, who had moved to India and left his house to them.

Nisma sounded calm and composed. She was curious to know about Kabir and Bhavi. She had a charming smile that reminded Bhavi of Devi Ma.

Suddenly, for a moment, Bhavi was carried away by the thoughts of Devi Ma. Nisma interrupted by offering a cup of ginger chai.

'It's been a very long time since I had such a wonderful cup of ginger chai,' said Bhavi, slowly sipping the tea.

Nisma informed Bhavi that Abdul had gone out and would ask him to come to their house once he returned.

Bhavi shook her head. 'No, no… nothing important. Just wanted to know the reason for his visit today. Abdul Bhaiyya and his friends had in search of Kabir.'

'Oh, that! Nothing to worry, dear. Some goods are being transported to Srinagar from Lahore. Abdul's boss had asked him to bring some men for help. That's why he was suggesting Kabir's name, I think. They give good money for such services. I will ask him about that when he comes back home.'

Bhavi sighed a relief and had her ginger tea in peace.

The two women started discussing their lives and babies for hours. Bhavi realised that with some strangers, you were just a conversation away from being close friends.

Kabir came back after an hour at dusk and Bhavi told him about the events that had unfolded. Kabir initially went to Abdul's house to find him, but he was not there. After putting in a lot of thought, he finally decided to visit their office.

The office building was just a street away from his place, and Kabir kept thinking that the time had finally come to shift to India as he started walking towards the office.

Now that Bhavi was alright and he had managed to earn some money via his rickshaw business, he thought it was time that they resumed their journey to India.

When he visited the office, there were a group of men discussing something seriously, and when Kabir introduced himself as Abdul's neighbour, they identified him. An old man among them called for Abdul.

He said to Kabir, 'Abdul will come in a few minutes. You can have a seat until then. You must be Kabir, right?'

'*Haan, Ji.* (Yes, Sir.)'

'And you are from?' the old man kept asking.

'From Baremullah.'

'How long were you there in Baremullah?'

Beads of sweat took form on Kabir's forehead and started dripping as the old man began asking questions regarding his whereabouts. Kabir's grandparents were from Baremullah. He used to visit them often during his school and college days until they passed away when he was in his third year. He thus remembered Baremullah very well. Though he was not a native of that place, he knew the town well, making him confident enough to tell everyone that he was from Baremullah.

After a short pause, Kabir answered, 'Till I finished my college.'

'So, then you must know the place pretty well,' the old man responded.

Abdul entered the room and waved at Kabir. Kabir waved back.

Abdul came near him, patting his shoulders and started introducing the old man in front of them as his boss.

He told him that the old man was a big landlord from Lahore, and now, he had expanded his business to Kashmir. Rice, wheat and other surplus grains, and vegetables were to be taken to the Srinagar market and they needed responsible men who could take up the work.

Abdul said, 'When they asked me some men for help, I told them about you. Day and night, I have seen you suffer riding the rickshaw just to earn some meagre amount. You have a family to take care of, and Boss will take care of you well.'

Abdul began praising his boss, and Kabir could see how proud he was working for him.

On seeing Kabir think and not sure about taking up the job, the old man offered Rs 100 for a single trip to Srinagar which might take a few days including his food and accommodation.

It was an offer that Kabir could not refuse. He thought even if he worked day and night with his rickshaw, it would take months to make such money. As they were going to start a new life upon reaching India, a little more cash would be very useful, he thought, and agreed with the old man.

It was the tenth of September, that day, Kabir was informed that the trip would be in five days. He headed back home and narrated to Bhavi all that had happened at the office. She was a little hesitant at first, but Kabir convinced her by saying, 'I will go for one such trip, then get the money, and we will vacate this place to start our journey to India.'

Bhavi asked, 'Is it truly necessary? Don't we have enough money now?'

'We have gathered enough in pennies. Yet a little more cash will come in handy. You know the situation outside. People are jobless, and the country's economy has collapsed. It is going to take a while for me to join back in the archaeology department. Until then, whatever comes our way, we must utilise it to the maximum.'

Bhavi understood the situation very well. Over the past few weeks, they had sent many letters to Kabir's dad in Firozpur, but there was not a single reply from him. They had no clue about the situation in Firozpur, and so, earning some cash beforehand was the best thing they could do.

That night, Kabir slept well after a very long time. New hope had blossomed in his heart. From running for survival and starving in hunger for days to finally sleeping peacefully under a roof, having food to eat for all three times a day, and a job in hand, they had come a long way. The only thing that was left for them, was to reach their place in India.

Chapter Fifteen

THE BEGINNING OF A NEVER-ENDING WAR

A week passed by, and the day of Kabir leaving for Srinagar finally came.

September 15, 1947

6:15 a.m.

Birds were chirping at a distance. Daylight slowly peeked in, and Kabir lazily woke up from his deep sleep. He had slept a little more than usual that day. As he checked the clock, he realised he was running short of time.

Kabir was asked to be at the office by 6:30 a.m. as the truck was scheduled to start at 7.

He took a quick shower and got dressed. He had already packed his bags the previous night. Bhavi had also been sleeping all that time. When she woke up, Kabir was ready to leave the house. Bhavi silently stood in one corner and watched Kabir doing his morning prayer routine. His eyes were closed, and as he bent, he uttered,

'Allahu Akbar.'

She asked him about his breakfast, to which he replied that everything would be taken care of by the company and asked her to take rest. As she stood at the entrance of their house holding one end of the door, Kabir walked into the bedroom and bid farewell to the kids who were sleeping.

He kissed them and gave a peck on Bhavi's cheek, too, before parting. He was happy and full of energy that morning. Bhavi waved back a goodbye and stood there, watching him slowly disappear into the streets. She knew that home would never be the same without him. They had planned to leave for India as soon as Kabir came back with the money.

Kabir went to the office and loaded the truck with the goods that were ready to be dispatched. He had help from five more men who introduced them as locals from Lahore.

The truck slowly started moving from Lahore. It was a long journey from there. The driver was Ajmal, who told them that he had decided to halt at Islamabad that night and continue the journey to Srinagar the next morning. Ajmal was a little over five feet tall and had a long beard almost touching his sternum. He had a pair of tiny green eyes that almost sunk inside his eyeballs.

Most of the goods inside the truck were in sealed wooden boxes. Only a few boxes with vegetables and fruits were open. A few hours went by, and Kabir kept admiring the roads and the greenery that they were crossing.

He realised that the chaos of partition was slowly settling down. His back began to hurt as the road became bumpy, and he decided to sleep on the floor, resting his head on his bag like a pillow. The truck was covered by a thick sheet to reduce the effects of the sun.

Kabir tried making conversation with the fellow members, but they didn't seem to respond well. Only one among them introduced himself as 'Ali' from Uri. He had come to Lahore after partition from

Uri. Kabir thought that he would have met the landlord while searching for a job for living.

Ali had a strikingly large, dark, brownish naevus on his nose. On a closer look, there were even few strands of hair coming out from that. Ali was thin built, his lips were cracked, and his hands were calloused. One could easily guess that he was a hard worker from his appearance.

He wondered why most of the men that his boss had recruited were from Kashmir. He was from Baremullah, and Ali was from Uri, which was a few kilometres away from Baremullah. Other than sharing his name and place, even Ali seemed to be an introvert who chose to remain silent most of the time.

Boredom struck Kabir, and he decided to take a nap to overcome that.

Hungry noises from his stomach woke him up around 3 p.m. The truck driver had not stopped for lunch. When asked, he replied that they couldn't afford to waste any more time as they were already running late and should be there in Islamabad in a few hours.

Kabir could no longer control his hunger and looked at the boxes behind him. One among them was filled with apples. He grabbed one from the box and took a bite. On seeing him, the rest of them began having apples as well. Kabir found the apple extremely sweet and juicy and was easily one of the best apples he had ever had.

The truck halted at Islamabad that night. Having had only apples since morning, all four men were craving some spicy food. They stayed that night in a small, dorm-like room and were served roti with mutton curry. Not just their stomachs but even their hearts were full that night.

Kabir had enough roti and even managed to take some more and preserve it for the next day's journey. He knew he wouldn't be able to survive with only apples for another day.

They went to sleep at late night and were woken up early in the morning around 4 a.m. The driver told them that the truck would start in 20 minutes. All four of them were half asleep, but still followed the orders of the driver. They quickly got ready, and the truck again began its arduous journey.

On their way from Islamabad to Srinagar, they were stopped by the army on the outskirts of the city. They checked the truck while enquiring about the contents of the box, and the driver told them that they were "Kashmiri apples". The army personnel quickly realised "the code" and left the truck unchecked.

Kabir, who had been noticing this conversation from the beginning, began to have a vivid doubt. *Abdul had said that they were transporting goods and vegetables from Lahore to Kashmir, but the driver says that they are Kashmiri apples. Why would they bring Kashmiri apples again to Kashmir?* He thought to himself.

Like the previous day, they were not given any breakfast. But Kabir managed with the rotis that he had snuck and even gave some to Ali who was awake, too.

Kabir started noticing that certain boxes were sealed airtight and had been packed in a way that could not be easily opened. This raised his suspicions. But the other four men looked innocent and harmless, sleeping on the way, still not fully awake from last night's sleep.

A few hours passed by, and Kabir pondering on all the possibilities that could happen. He just couldn't connect the dots. If they were to cause any sort of harm to him, then why not harm him at his place itself? Why transport him to Srinagar and lie to him about their true intentions?

He kept thinking, trying to conclude any of these questions, but failed. The truck came to a sudden halt. He got thrown to the front a bit. Kabir looked outside, it was bright and sunny. It was as if he remembered this place.

He peeked a little more and glanced at the mountains and valleys ahead of him. He quickly realised that it was Abbottabad after seeing a waterfall at some distance. It was the same waterfall that they had stumbled upon five years back.

The last time, when he was here, he was here with Ibhrahim, Daya, and Vimal. *Why on earth is the driver stopping at Abbottabad?* He thought.

He went to the other side to notice that they were getting into some kind of guarded territory. As the driver stopped at the entrance, he exchanged a few words with the armed guards outside, after which, they let their truck in. The guards were not in military uniforms but were instead dressed like normal adults, the only difference being they were vigilant and armed.

As the truck entered the perimeter, the other guys woke up as well. All of them looked clueless regarding this new place. After continuing the journey for a while, the truck finally came to a halt in the centre of that place. It was like a huge ground surrounded by tents all around. The driver jumped out of the truck and asked Kabir and his men to come out and begin unloading the boxes from the truck.

Kabir came out of the truck and looked around the place. There were numerous people with tents pegged one after another. Everyone seemed to be busy with work. Kabir came to the conclusion that he had fallen into some kind of trouble. It's just that he did not realise the intensity of the trouble. He kept looking around and wondered what was happening.

At a distance, he could see that some men were cooking in big vessels enough to feed a large population. Ahead of them was a group of people practising shooting with rifles. The problem was much more serious than he had thought.

The driver interrupted him by yelling loudly that he was not helping them unload the packages. Kabir went back to help them and when he asked the driver what place this was, the driver bluntly replied to him that 'Boss will answer all questions.'

Nobody even mentioned his name. He was just called as their "Boss". Kabir kept thinking as he helped them with the boxes.

When all the packages were unloaded from the truck, they were asked to be kept inside the first tent by a man who was also armed with a rifle. As Kabir picked an apple box and struggled to carry it to the tent, he could hear the truck leaving the place. He immediately placed the apples on the ground and ran towards the truck, and yelled, 'Ajmal!'

Unfortunately, he was stopped by that same guard who ordered him to do as he was instructed.

Not knowing what to do and being heavily outnumbered, he decided to stay calm and not create a ruckus.

September 16, 1947

Abbottabad

2 p.m.

After they had arranged the packages, they were asked to go near tent number 3 for lunch. The lunch was served to them on plates, and they were told that the Boss would meet them in the evening. Until then, they were asked to attend the physical training classes in the ground.

Having travelled continuously for two days, in addition to not getting proper food and sleep had made them profoundly tired. Meanwhile, Ali had begun to open up to Kabir. He was in the same state as Kabir, equally confused and scared. The rest of the men had formed groups among themselves. They had friends with some of the men who were already stationed in that place, and the activities happening there did not take them by surprise.

Only Kabir and Ali were the odd ones out. After lunch, as they headed to the ground in the centre, they crossed tent 1, where they had kept all the boxes arranged. As they went nearby, Kabir peeked inside and found two men opening the sealed boxes. Before he could see what was inside the box, the two men became alert and closed the tent.

Kabir, along with Ali and his other truck mates, went to the ground. An officer greeted him. He was the only one in uniform inside the whole camp. He was surely an officer; Kabir could sense that with his tone and behaviour. But the uniform that he wore was a bit peculiar, and he had never seen that before.

The officer asked them to introduce themselves and instructed them to stay physically active and alert in the following days to come.

'You will be given enough food to eat and pieces of equipment to train. All you need to do is co-operate with us here and do as you are instructed to do. All six of you will stay in a single tent along with a few others in tent number 12. Your day starts at 5 a.m. and ends at 10 p.m. You cannot contact anybody outside, and you are prohibited to leave this place without prior permission from us. This training will go on only for a few weeks. By Allah's grace, it will be over much before that also. When everything is over, you can go back to your homes and will be paid good money. It's a lifetime opportunity to serve your country and your people. Pakistan Zindabad. Now you can go to your respective tents. Boss will come and meet you.' His words were crisp, sharp, and fearful. He had the tone of an army man. In his voice, they could sense a burning desire to avenge something.

While going back to the tent, Kabir managed to sneak inside tent number 1 while passing by. He carefully went inside the tent and checked the boxes. To his surprise, the boxes were packed with rifles, pistols, and bombs. He was taken aback when he realised that these were the goods that they were transporting from Lahore. And all this time, Kabir and the other men were travelling with these weapons in the truck. Suddenly, he could hear some footsteps approaching the tent, so, quickly took a pistol out of one of the boxes and hid it inside his kurta.

Before the man could enter the tent, Kabir left the other way without anyone noticing. Back in the tent, when no one was there, he managed to bury the pistol wrapped in a cloth nearby his tent.

Chapter Sixteen

KASHMIRI FREEDOM

September 16, 1947

Abbottabad

6 p.m.

In the evening, a man came to their tent and asked them to assemble in front of the tent marked 01, upon the order of their boss. Only he could give them all the answers that they had been seeking. The six men hurried to tent 01 to find their boss having a conversation with the officer.

They abruptly stopped their conversation on seeing those men, and the officer left after shaking hands with the boss. The superiors had no names inside the premises. Their boss was always referred to as the "Boss" and the army man as "The Officer".

Kabir had no clue of the names of even his fellow men. After sending the Officer out, the Boss sat on his chair and began observing the faces of those five men. He watched all of them closely and patted his thighs. With a loud 'Ahem,' he began to speak.

'I believe all of you will be having a lot of questions to ask me. I will clear them in a while. But before that, remember this one thing. Every man will get a chance in his lifetime to fight for his country and his people, and to be selfless in the process for the sake of his brothers. Because of that one act of yours, your country will remember you forever, and people will thank you for the decades to come. This is one such chance for you all.

A brief history of Stand Still Agreement

After the British decided to give India independence, there were more than 500 provinces still ruled by Kings and Zamindars. They were given three options. One, to join India; two, to join Pakistan; or three, they could remain as an independent province. It was up to their wish to decide. While most of the provinces agreed to join India, there was the state of Kashmir, with a Muslim majority people, ruled by a Hindu King Raja Hari Singh, which did not agree. The king was unwilling to join either India or Pakistan, and he signed the Standstill Agreement, that is, to remain neutral and not to join both the sides for the time being. Pakistan signed this agreement, while India did not. Pakistan signed this agreement in the sense that they could not claim Kashmir as theirs. Whereas India never signed it. This angered Pakistan. Both India and Pakistan were angling to assimilate Jammu and Kashmir into their respective territories.

Lord Mountbatten and Sardar Vallabhai Patel negotiated with Hari Singh to join India. But Raja never gave heed to it. He was not ready to join either of the sides.

Anti-Maharaja protests

Moreover, Maharaja's rule in Kashmir was not liked by a group of Muslims, as they were denied with official posts and opportunities just because they were Muslims. Those Muslims thought that they were not treated as fairly as the Hindus were. Also, they believed that the Muslims were dealt with harshly and with an iron fist. This led to them to form rebel groups and the frequent outbreaks of rebellions. They were called "Anti-Maharaja protests". This created a constant fuss at Raja Hari Singh's court. Moreover, after the partition, he could not keep an eye on the porous border of Kashmir in case of any external aggression. Within 12 days of signing the standstill agreement, Pakistan wrote a warning note to the Maharaja, quoting, 'The time has come for Maharaja of Kashmir that he must make his choice, and to choose Pakistan. Should Kashmir fail to join Pakistan, the gravest possible trouble will inevitably ensue.'

On the other hand, Nehru and Gandhi wanted Kashmir to join India. But Raja disliked becoming part of India, which was democratised, or even Pakistan, which is an Islamic state.

'Now, listen to me closely. As you all are aware, it's been almost a month since we got a separate nation for ourselves. We fought for it with all our might. And here, we are enjoying the fruits of our years of struggle. But our fellow brothers from Kashmir have suffered enough. Raja Hari Singh is not one among us, and he would never consider them as his people. They have been fighting for a while now, and it's high time for us to help them. Kashmir belongs to us, and we must fight for it. You must prepare yourself in the following weeks and be ready. Whoever is not interested can go back to their respective homes. I'm warning you all once again, the cowards who do not want to serve our nation can go back to their homes before the sun comes up tomorrow and never come face to face with me in your life. If, at all, I see your face ever again, remember, you are a lump of dead meat. The rest who decide to stay back, trust me, you will never regret becoming a part of our brotherhood. I will meet you all tomorrow morning and brief you about our plan. Go to your tents now.'

The other men went back to the tent, but Ali and Kabir still stood there, speechless unable to digest all that they had heard. They were recruited for the job of porters and now they were being asked to be a part of a militia.

Boss, on seeing those two men standing like statues, commanded with an air of authority, 'You two, I said leave the tent now.'

Ali and Kabir finally came out of the trance and left the place. As they were heading towards their tent, they continued to remain silent and did not speak a word.

At night, jammed with more than 10 men in a single tent, Kabir and Ali were lying next to each other, staring at the tent's roof. Kabir looked around and found that everyone was fast asleep, except Ali. There was occasional loud snoring, breaking the deep silence inside the tent. Kabir whispered to Ali, 'Not feeling sleepy?' Ali was not really in a mood to respond and just said 'Going to.'

This was followed by another few minutes of silence until he finally opened up, saying, 'I have two daughters waiting for me at Lahore. All of us have already seen the dark face of the partition, and just when we were settling and looking to begin a new life, this happened. I'm not a brave warrior or a country soldier. I'm just a father who is looking to give a good life to his daughters. I don't want to fight someone else's wars while I'm already fighting mine.'

'I have a daughter, too. She is 2 months old.'

'Those times were the best. Once they grow up you will miss holding them in your arms, holding them like they are the greatest treasure that you had ever found in your life.'

A tiny smile creased Kabir's cheeks and every bit of him wanted to hold Indya as long as he could and never leave her out of his arms. He wanted to be there for her in every step of her life. There were so many things that he had planned for her. If not for this chaos of partition, they would have been in their hometown, Firozpur, happily celebrating Indya and India every day.

After some time, Kabir asked Ali again, 'What are you going to do tomorrow?'

And after there was no response, he realised that Ali had also drifted to sleep. Now, he was all alone inside the tent.

He slowly turned to look at Ali's face and was taken aback suddenly. He saw Daya's face in front of him. It gave him chills for a moment. He did not want to look back at the memories, at least not yet. He shut his eyes, quickly turning back.

After a point, he couldn't breathe well and felt choked, as if the oxygen inside the tent had depleted. He emerged out of the tent for some fresh air and found the company of crickets chirping in the background and the rustling of leaves. He was surrounded by darkness everywhere except for the gleaming moonlight, at the end of which he sensed was to be the waterfall.

He was able to vaguely hear the sound of the water splashing on the rocks on close observation. The sound was mild yet mesmerising.

The cold winds were freezing as he locked his hands and slowly immersed his mind in the situation that he was in. Overpowering all the background noise was his heart pounding restlessly. He realised that he had been hallucinating, but for a second, it seemed so real. The face he just saw made all their memories come back flooding in.

He thought about their last dinner at Daya's house, and how his childhood at Firozpur was nothing but pages of roaming around the village and playing hide and seek with Daya.

After his death, Kabir felt as if a piece of his heart had been taken away from him, and he was left with heartache for a lifetime which no one could heal, a pang of never-ending guilt for leaving him behind in that way that nothing can mend. But he knew that he had to come to terms with the fact that Daya had left. Daya had left, months back, yet his memories were etched deeply inside Kabir's heart.

As he kept thinking of Daya, tears rolled down his cheeks, and wiping them, he made up his mind and decided to be strong enough, at least until he took Bhavi, Abhi and Indya to India. He was their only hope. Abhi was his Daya now.

Suddenly, he heard a loud whistle coming from his right side. He turned to notice that the armed guards were taking shifts and roaming the place even at night.

The guard flashed a torchlight on his face and signalled him to go inside his tent, and Kabir did so. Back at the tent, he didn't have the guts to look back at Ali even though he badly wanted to. He closed his eyes. As he gave it a lot of thought, a few things were clear to him. One, he could never be a part of something like this. He could never do this to his country. He loved India more than he loved his religion.

Two, he could leave tomorrow, otherwise he would not know their plan. He knew deep in his heart that he had to do something about this rebellion. He had to tell somebody about this plan, somebody who could pass this piece of information to the Indian government, so that the attack could be avoided.

It was impossible to contact someone outside from here. So, he started thinking of the possibilities to escape this place.

I will hear their plan tomorrow, and then, escape this place somehow, he thought to himself and slowly drifted to sleep.

The next morning, Kabir woke up to the cold breeze brushing his hair and face from one side of the tent. The tent had been already opened and all the men near him had woken up.

Kabir realised that he had overslept and quickly got outside the tent. He saw the waterfall which he had heard the previous night.

The air was fresh, and he could hear the chorus of birds flying above him. At a distance, he saw the other men standing in a queue with plates in their hands for the morning breakfast.

He went in the opposite direction where they had the washroom facility. There was a huge tank in the centre filled with water up to the brim. He found men standing beside the tank and some taking baths, some washing clothes.

He searched for a bucket and found one in a withered condition in one of the corners. He took it, filled it with water from the tank, and poured it over his head. It was cold. Still, he wouldn't stop and continued to pour more buckets of water in that way.

The strange thing about this brotherhood was that nobody would talk to anybody. They remained silent most of the time and would only speak when asked to. Kabir wondered where Ali was, wiping his head with a dry towel. He had not seen Ali since he had woken up.

He changed his clothes and headed to the open dining area. It was already late, and by the time Kabir was in the line, they closed the vessels and told the few men who were standing in the queue that the food was over.

Nobody questioned and the few men standing in the queue left the place. Kabir now realised that he had to wake up early to get food here. He found a water pot nearby. He drank almost half a litre of water in one go and filled his stomach.

He heard the whistles again, this time coming from the centre of the ground. It was time for assembly and practice. Kabir slowly made his way to the ground. On his way, he stumbled upon a few guards carrying a man's body.

Two of them were holding his legs and another guard was holding his head. Kabir was shocked to see blood dripping from the man's body.

The guards crossed by him, and Kabir turned back noticing the blood on the man's kurta. He took one last look at the man's face and found dark brown naevus on his nose.

It was Ali.

Chapter Seventeen

THE PLAN

September 17, 1947

8 a.m.

Kabir's only companion there had been killed.

He had been murdered by the people who had brought him here in the first place. He now realised how treacherous these people were.

Maybe Ali tried to escape that night, or he wanted to leave for home to see his daughters. Kabir would never know what really happened that night unless Ali woke up and narrated what had happened.

He also thought that whatever might have been the reason, how dare they kill him for that? Those men began the wars, stating that they wanted to help their people, but would they go to the extent of killing their own men for the same?

'How foolish have men become in the name of religion!' Thinking about all this made Kabir frustrated and angry. But he was helpless. He was a single man against an army of assassins.

He wished he had his father near him right now to knock some sense into the minds of these men. He felt that it was Kashmir's decision to join India or Pakistan, or to stay independent. Who were they to wage a war against them for acquiring them?

By the time he was processing all this, all men were lined up in the centre of the ground.

The Officer had come, and he was speaking, rather screaming, giving out commands which failed to enter Kabir's mind in spite of being loud.

Kabir's thoughts kept drifting. Would Ali's family be notified about his death? How would his two daughters take it?

The incident that he had just witnessed neither broke him nor made him sad; he was only angry. Kabir had come too far to feel the pain of every death that he encountered.

Death didn't impact him as much as it would have earlier. By now, he had almost become immune to deaths. This was the fifth or sixth time he had witnessed someone close to him pass away since the partition line was announced and had lost count of the deaths. He remembered the last time he saw Ali's face. He saw Daya's face on him, and now, he, too, was dead, just like Daya.

He understood that the situation was going out of control, and these people were way more dangerous than he had thought. He decided to put his escaping plan on hold. He never wanted to take the chance of leaving this place after seeing Ali. He was certain that what had happened to Ali that day could easily happen to him tomorrow.

He remembered the Boss telling them the previous night that if anybody wanted to leave, they should leave before the sun came up today, and he looked up above to see the sun shining brighter like never before right on his face. It was too late now.

The Officer in the front continued giving instructions, and Kabir was standing in the last row of men. That day, each of the men in the camp were assigned with numbers. The numbers were mentioned on the piece of cloth that was supposed to be tied above their kurta like a vest.

The Officer was given the number 1.

Kabir was given the number 149. And they were all instructed to call each other with their assigned numbers only. This solved their issue of not calling everyone with their names.

They were divided into groups, and Kabir and a few men were ordered to learn about grenades that day. They were assigned to a man, Number 5, and he took them to one corner of the territory under the shade of a cedar tree.

There, on one side, were boxes filled with hand grenades.

Number 5 took one and started explaining the basics of a grenade. He nicknamed the grenade as 'military confetti".

He went on, 'These are designed to seriously maim anyone in its path by throwing thousands of metal shards hundreds of feet per second. It can potentially injure anyone within 10 to 20 metres' radius, and the shrapnel can reach hundreds of metres, but its effectiveness decreases with increase in the distance.'

He switched the hand grenade to his right hand and continued, 'There are many types of grenades. What you all will be given is the explosive one and the smoke screening one.'

There are designed this way like a pineapple in order to have a better grip while throwing it. What you see outside is the metal casing filled with explosive material inside. And this pin that you see here is the trigger pin. Once you pull the trigger, it's only a matter of seconds before it gets detonated.'

The Officer who passed by the training group added, 'You need to be very careful while using them. You know, poorly trained soldiers sometimes pull the trigger and drop the grenade at their own feet.'

He laughed as if this was some kind of a joke and left the place. Except the Officer and Number 5, nobody else laughed.

Kabir went nuts in this whole process. He was used to shooting pictures of ancient, recovered sites while working under the archaeological survey of India, but now, he had to learn how to throw a grenade. Life had gone 180-degree upside down for him.

Number 5 further continued the session, saying, 'There are two things that are extremely important while throwing a grenade. One, have a target before you pull the trigger. Have a target and locate your enemy, because a grenade doesn't identify whether it's a friend or a foe. Once the trigger is pulled, and if you have not located the enemy yet, it's a disaster for sure. And two, most importantly, once the grenade has left your hands, take cover immediately. I mean, immediately. I cannot stress this enough.'

After a while, the men were taken under a shelter and Number 5 gave a live demonstration by pulling the trigger and throwing it of at a distance which was followed by a loud thud. Few men screamed like children and Kabir felt as if his ear drums had been shattered. There was this excruciating pain on his right ear and his left ear was totally blocked. He could hear only people mumbling and it took a while for his ear block to clear.

The session went on till noon and was followed by lunch break.

Again, men lined up in queue for the food and so did Kabir. He sat alone and started having his roti, thinking about what he had learnt just now, and what had happened to Ali in the morning. He was adamant to not let that happen to him.

The roti was hard to tear and rubbery when chewed, the pickle that they had given with it had a watery consistency and was way too salty. Each one of them was also given a small cup of tea.

Kabir gave up on the roti and pickle and started to have the roti dipped in tea. Though not palatable, he could at least chew it easily now. The only day's good food was served to them was the days when their Boss or the Officer was having food with them.

Lunch break was followed by a briefing session on how to use shot guns. Men who had never seen a gun in real life were given one and were asked to train with it.

Then, evening came, and the Boss had come that day as well to meet them. The group of men were asked to sit in a large semicircle, facing the Boss in the front. He was joined by the Officer, and they began narrating the plan for the attack.

September 17, 1947

6 p.m.

'Good to see all of you,' said the Boss. 'You are sitting here with us this evening. It means that you have chosen to stay back and fight for our cause. Let me congratulate each and every one of you for taking this decision. You are going to make your country and family proud. I can see that all of you had been given a vest with a number. Remember, you are always supposed to wear them. Wear it every time you step out of your tent in the morning and remove it only when the day is over and when you are going to sleep. Wear it every day and wear it with pride. Now, the Officer, will brief us on our plan. Listen to him closely.'

Began the Officer, 'Good evening, everyone. I hope today's session went on very well for you. Let us all keep up this practice and give our full potential to fight for this noble cause. All of you have come to us as men but will return to your home as warriors. When the right day comes, we will begin our attack.

'We will start by infiltrating into Muzaffarabad on Day 1. We are actually on the borders of Pakistan and India, in Abbottabad, and are only a few kilometres away from Muzaffarabad.

Muzaffarabad is our entry point, and then, we will enter Uri. There, our brothers from Kashmir will join us. Together, we will become undefeatable and from there we will make our way towards Mahura. There, lies the most crucial step of our plan. The power station supplying electricity to Srinagar is in Mahura. We will destroy the power station and cut the power supply to Srinagar. By then, the news would have reached the Maharaja's ears, and he will regret the mistake that he made.

'Slowly, we will gather all our men and supporters and move towards Baremullah. And then, finally, from there, we will march towards the city and capture Srinagar and its king, Raja Hari Singh. We will show him our power, and finally, make him choose Pakistan.'

This speech was followed by a 'Pakistan Zindabad' chorus from his men.

The crowd was asked to disperse, and it was followed by dinner and after that, all men were instructed to go inside their respective tents as that day's events came to an end.

Before going to sleep, Kabir opened his bag and took out his Quran, the one that he had gifted to Bhavi and offered a small prayer to Ali and his family. That's the least he could do.

After the prayer, he was too exhausted mentally and physically to stay awake and drifted to sleep instantly.

September 18, 5 a.m.

Kabir woke up the next day. and that day was followed by another session of hands-on training with grenades and shotguns. This time, a few men were called to come forward, were given one grenade each, and were ordered to throw it.

Kabir escaped being selected by avoiding eye contact with the trainer. He just stood there among the audience and witnessed the men with trembling hands as they held the grenade for the first time in their lives.

In contrast to these men, some were very much interested in this training process. They were the first ones to wake up every day with high *josh* (enthusiasm) and they took part in all the training and prepared for the war as if it was their own war. They even idolised the Officer and their Boss and shouted, 'Pakistan Zindabad' in chorus whenever it was needed. And they were the last to sleep.

The hatred they all had grown in their hearts towards India, the Hindu nation, by then in their eyes were on full blooms.

Kabir couldn't do anything other than pitying them for how narrow minded they were.

It was followed by another session where their endurance was tested by making them run around the camp site 8 times. No one could escape this, and all men were made to run. Some struggled to even walk after five rounds panting heavily.

A few gave up after six but were forced to complete the run by the trainer who was at the centre of the ground, charging on anyone who stopped in the middle.

The endurance test was over, and some passed, while some failed. This was taken as the criteria and the men who completed the test within the stipulated time were regrouped together as the "star team".

Kabir could not finish it after the seventh round and was taken into the latter team. From that day, they were trained separately. The star team had access to the more advanced weapons, while Kabir and his men were only given the grenades. They were trained to walk and climb the mountainous terrain with a weight on their shoulders.

This went on for a few more days. Every day, they began their training with physical exercise and running. And each day had many sessions. They had introductory classes, hands-on training sessions with the same weapon, and various tips and tactics to cross the porous border of Kashmir. Their day ended with their Boss or their

Officer giving motivational speeches.

September 27, 11 p.m.

That night, after the practice session, Kabir sat outside his tent with his Quran and stared at the waterfall at a distance. The waterfall had been crossing his mind and his eyes for quite some time now.

A slow fresh breeze hit him, flipping the pages of Quran. Kabir quickly closed it tight and noticed a small note peeping just outside the edges of the book. He slid it away and noticed an address written on it. It was the address of his friend, Vimal, whom he had met during their road trip. He had written his address in a piece of paper and given it to him many years back.

Every memory of Vimal came to him all at once. He continued glancing at the waterfall and remembered Vimal Adityan, the tall guy with round spectacles.

He looked at the address again and he knew deep at his heart that Vimal would help him in a situation like this; after all, he was Vimal. Also, he was a very influential man in Srinagar. His father was a minister at Raja Hari Singh's court and Kabir was sure that he would have connections with the Indian army.

Kabir got an idea of contacting Vimal.

A few more days passed by, and Kabir noticed the pattern inside the camp.

Ajmal arrived once every four days with a bunch of people and boxes of food supplies and equipment. Kabir and Ali were dropped off at that site on September 16, after which Ajmal came after four days, i.e., on September 20, and then, again on September 24. So, if Kabir's calculations were right, then he must come on September 28, which was the following day.

He was the only one going in and out of the camp site regularly. If at all there was any slightest chance of contacting the outside world, it should be through him, he thought.

While travelling from Lahore to Abbottabad in Ajmal's truck, Kabir had noticed one thing about Ajmal. He was very fond of money and would do anything just to get some. When they left Lahore, Boss had given Ajmal some money for getting the men food for the next two days of travel. But Ajmal left them all starving and kept the excess money to himself.

So, Ajmal would help him if Kabir gave him some money. But he would never agree to reveal the happenings of this place to the outside world that would tamper their mission.

So, it had to be through Ajmal, but he shouldn't know the real intention.

September 28, 11 a.m.

Since morning, Kabir was anxious, waiting for the arrival of Ajmal's truck. At 11, they had a 10-minute tea break and that's when Ajmal's truck came inside the camp. As usual, Kabir snuck away from the crowd and when Ajmal got down from the truck, he quickly dragged him inside one of his tents.

He quickly closed the covers of the tent and gave Ajmal a small piece of cloth wrapped like a ball. Inside, he had kept the last bit of money that was left with him and pleaded Ajmal to bring him two postcards the next time he came inside the campus.

He explained it to Ajmal that, his wife had just birthed their new-born baby and while leaving home, he had told her that he will only be out for a few days. But it had been more than a week and she would panic.

'I really need to send a letter to her and tell her I'm fine. Please, help me this one time, Ajmal, please,' he begged.

Okay, I will help you. You give me her address; I will write and send her one,' said Ajmal.

'No… No. it has to be from me. I have to write it. Only then she will recognise my handwriting and know it's from me.'

'You don't understand, it's not that easy. I'm not allowed to bring anything from outside to you, brother. If I get caught, the Boss will never spare me.'

'Please, Ajmal, please. Don't say no. I have given you all that I had. It's just a postcard, it will do no harm.'

'Why can't you ask Boss? if it is truly necessary, he will definitely help you.'

'Both of us know that's never going to happen,' said Kabir.

There was a moment of silence between the two men, and they could hear someone from the outside shouting Ajmal's name.

'Sorry, brother, I have to leave.'

Kabir held his hand and giving him the money pouch, pleaded him for one last time.

'Ajmal, please do this one favour to me and I will give you more money once I receive my pay from the Boss after this mission is over.'

Ajmal shouted back at him, saying 'I'm coming,' and replied to Kabir, 'Okay. I will help you this time,' after putting in a lot of thought and quickly left the tent hiding the money pouch inside his kurta.

Kabir felt happy on this small accomplishment and continued his way to the session where he was asked to go four rounds around the ground as punishment for coming late to the session.

Kabir took their orders and completed four rounds and got totally exhausted.

That noon, they were served the same hard roti with pickle and tea. Some men were protesting this unpalatable food in the food counter. But nobody took it into consideration.

When the evening came, the Boss had arrived, and a few men had gathered all their guts and went and spoke to him regarding the food that they were being served. They argued, 'Doing physical activity all day long, everyone is famished, and this roti and tea cannot suffice our hunger.'

The Boss found their complaints legit and promised to do something regarding it.

Chapter Eighteen

LETTER TO A FRIEND

Four days later, Kabir was again looking forward to Ajmal's return. He counted the days and every day seemed like an entire month passed by.

One day, Kabir was the last one to have dinner. He came back to the tent, thinking about the day's events, and as he was crossing by tent number one, he overheard the Officer discussing something serious with the other trainers. He slowed a bit and tried to eavesdrop without being noticed.

'Officer, even though we are training day and night, will it be sufficient to take over Kashmir?' a trainer asked.

'Do not worry, my friend. We are 30000 men strong.'

'30000 men? We hardly have 1000 here.' The trainer sounded flabbergasted.

'No, my friend, did you actually think we would attack Kashmir with just a thousand men? Only a fool would do that. We have planned and gathered as many forces as possible. We are going to attack Kashmir on three fronts: the Gilgit front, the Srinagar front, and the Jammu front. We belong to the Srinagar front, and each front consists of 10 units of 1000 each, making 10000 all together for a single front. Thus, in total, we are an army of 30000 men. Not just this, with the help of the local tribal people, we are launching small attacks here and there throughout Kashmir to disperse the Jammu and Kashmir forces that will be stationed at the major points of the state. Once the J&K forces are dispersed, we will attack and capture all three major towns of Kashmir—Srinagar, Jammu, and Gilgit through the main roadways. The little J&K forces that are left behind on the major roads would tremble upon seeing us and would be taken aback by the element of surprise. They would be helpless and vulnerable without any external help. That's when we will hit them. We will hit them once and hit them hard and bring Kashmir back home.'

'This sounds like a victory plan, Officer. But just one thing, how are we going to join the men on D-Day?'

'Every front has one major like me and ten junior commissioner officers like you, who all will dress up as tribals and local men and become one with them.'

When this conservation was going on, Kabir heard a few trainers at a distance coming toward him, so he slowly backed away and ran to his tent.

In the tent, he kept thinking about what he had just heard. So, now he realised that this was not just a small rebellion, rather massive on its scale. He could not just stand there doing nothing.

The fact that they had planned to launch an attack from three fronts seemed like a big thing, but he knew all these were scary only until there was an element of surprise. When that was taken away, they could be prepared for what is coming for them. Kabir was sure that he had to somehow convey all that information to Vimal when he came there, or at least he hoped that he would come without any doubt.

All of Kabir's hopes and efforts were chained to one event and that was whether Vimal was going to come there for him or not. Even if he really came, how was Kabir ever going to escape from that place and meet Vimal at the waterfall? All that Kabir thought about day and night was the answer to this one question. He had been delaying his escape from that place only to gather more information on the events that had been planned. Still, even if he tried to escape, it should be worth it, and it would be worthwhile if only he was able to contact Vimal.

Finally, the day came when Ajmal was supposed to come.

October 2, 2 p.m.

The truck was late that particular day, and Kabir was having lunch when the truck came rushing inside the gates. It quickly came to a thumped stop at one end of the ground. It was parked in a different place from where it would be usually parked.

Kabir washed his plates and quickly made his way to the ground. To his surprise, he found somebody else jumping off the truck. He was well built and had a wheatish complexion with a short, neatly groomed beard. He wore a khaki kurta and had a small bag hanging on one side of his shoulders.

The trainers when they saw him called him out by his name. 'Hey, Farooq,' and hugged him after exchanging a few words. Everybody knew him here. He had come in place of Ajmal.

Kabir stood speechless for a moment. All his hope came shattering down.

Farooq moved the goods from the truck to the tents and kept looking around. It was as if he was looking out for somebody. Kabir, who was noticing him from a distance, finally gave in and decided to ask him about the postcards.

He went near him and offered his help in moving the boxes from the truck and whispered to him, 'Did Ajmal give you any postcards?'

The man stayed silent. There was no reply.

He asked him again, this time seeing looking him in the eye, but still, there was no reply.

When the Officer saw Farooq, he came by and called him to have lunch. Farooq was hesitant at first. He wouldn't talk to him either. But the Officer insisted him about having lunch and took him forcefully to the lunch place.

Kabir followed him there and saw him asking for one more roti in sign language. That's when he realised that he was deaf and mute.

Oh, God, how on Earth am I going to explain to him what I want? Kabir thought to himself and went and sat beside him and drew a rectangle postcard in air and tried to explain it to him what he really wanted with gestures.

Farooq finally nodded and realised he was the one. He looked around to check if anyone was noticing and grabbed two postcards from his sling bag.

Kabir signalled to him that he would be back in five minutes and left the place.

Farooq nodded, and also took out a pen from his bag and gave it to him before he left.

Kabir came inside his tent, took out his Quran and placed the two postcards inside it. He sent a quick prayer and began to write his first letter to Vimal Adityan.

He knew it had to be fast and crisp, because his mates could come in any minute.

He thus began,

*Hello, Vimal. **I'm** good. Hope you are in good health.*

*If at all you **need** anything, let me know.*

*I hope I will be **of** some **help** to you.*

*We shall meet at **our place** soon and take a dive one more time.*

Please *convey my regards to your family.*

I remembered your birthday is on **OCTOBER 21**

May you be blessed with all that you ever wish for.

happy birthday to you ***my one and only beloved friend.***

Love,

Kabir.

Kabir wrote a short letter that carried the message in it, which would escape the eyes of whoever read them casually. He went on to darken certain words more than one time, making them more prominent than others.

He flipped the postcard to the other side and entered the address from the small note that Vimal had given five years back. Suddenly, Kabir had this strange doubt whether Vimal would be still living in the same place as mentioned here. A few seconds passed by, and Kabir decided to send them anyhow and just wish for his arrival on that day.

After finishing the letter, he peeked outside the tent to check on Farooq, who was still eating the rotis.

Then he took the second postcard and began writing 'To my dearest Bhavi Ma.'

The mere thought of her name brought smiles to his face and peace to his soul. It had been this way since they had first met at the flower market. They say love is great when it's new, but in their case, it had been ageing well like wine. As days went by, their love for each other grew bounds and leaps.

Then, he suddenly remembered; she was actually Shabnam now. Using her real name might lead to unwanted troubles.

To my dearest Shabnam,

Hope you and the kids are doing good.

I'm doing fine here.

I know you would be missing me,

I'm missing you here more than ever.

I told you I will be back in a week or so

but it's taking a little more time here.

Nevertheless, when my work is over,

I will come running to you.

The fact that I'm this far away from you

at this point in life agonises me every night.

I dream of the day when I can hold you and

our baby in my arms and never leave you both, ever.

I will come home soon, honey

And we will move to our home soon and

begin our life on a fresh slate.

This time, we are going to make it.

Take good care of Hussain. Convey my regards to him.

He is the son we always asked for.

Love you to the ~~moon~~ Sun and back.

Can't wait to see you.

Love

Kabir.

While he was writing the address on the letter to Bhavi, he heard a quick and loud horn honking from the truck. It was time. He scribbled the address on the card, blew a quick kiss, and brought the card to the truck.

When the truck was making a turn in the ground, Kabir went to the other side and managed to give Farooq the two cards and requested him to post them without fail. He hoped that he would understand what he meant.

After the truck passed through the gates, Kabir kept staring at it, for it had the most important message that had to be delivered.

A trainer spotted Kabir standing and staring at the gates and yelled at him at the top of his voice for wasting time. He hurriedly joined his team seated under a Mulberry tree at the right corner of the ground. That noon, there was this session on how to give first aid in case of any bullet injury to the limbs and the vital parts of the body and the importance of helping each other in times of need was stressed enough.

At night, Kabir noticed the moonlight streaming inside his tent through a hole and remembered a day during his college days with Bhavi. He had snuck into her house at night, and both of them had laid in their attic, staring at the moon, so brilliant that it made the stars go pale.

They were discussing about the strange feeling that one got sometimes when they met somebody and spoke for the first time, but it felt like they have known each other all along; how with some people one easily became attached, maybe because they came from the same stars.

'Then, I think maybe Vimal came from my star,' Kabir had replied.

'Oh, Vimal? Your road trip friend? What about me, then?' Bhavi asked him as she pinched his ears to the point where Kabir cried out loud, 'No, no... I met him for the first time that day and it seemed like I knew him forever, just like what you were saying now.'

Bhavi still hadn't left his ears and he ended up shouting, 'Yeah... yeah... you too... from the same star.'

Kabir gave a soft giggle as he was dreaming with his eyes wide open and finally went to sleep.

The vigorous training sessions continued for the days to come. They were taught how to climb mountains, how to make their way in the mountainous terrains, how to defend themselves in case of an attack, and how to injure the enemy in case of combat.

Days passed by, and all that Kabir could do was just hope that Vimal received his letter.

October 20, 11 a.m.

The truck came inside the gates with Farooq as the driver. The day when Kabir gave money to Ajmal was the last day that he saw Ajmal.

Thenceforth, only Farooq came in place of Ajmal. One time, he even signalled Farooq, asking whether he had sent the letters, but he never responded.

On his visit that day, Kabir was in his session on mountain climbing and something peculiar happened. One, it was not his usual date. Two, a group of women got down from the truck, some with baggage in hands and a few with kids on their waists. Kabir, who was at a distance, was noticing all these and the women were taken to the food preparation area.

'Didn't you all complain about the food to the Boss? That's why they are here,' interrupted the trainer.

The women had been brought from many areas of Pakistan to prepare food for the militia.

When it was time for lunch, Kabir as usual took his plates and was standing in a queue.

While he was on his way to the counter, he heard two trainers passing by, mumbling, 'The feast before the battle,' pointing toward the food that was kept. He soon realised that the day of the attack was not far away, and it was very near. It might even be tomorrow, but Kabir had asked Vimal to come here only on October 21 (the next day).

Flooded with all this information on his mind, he noticed that at noon, a jaggery sweet was distributed to each one of them along with the usual roti. Men rejoiced like kids, for it was the first time in weeks that they were tasting something sweet. Their taste buds had partially gone dead and the jaggery sweet was reviving those.

Kabir was overjoyed since that was his favourite sweet and eagerly kept moving forward as the queue slowly reduced one by one. He noticed men commenting that the sweet was delicious. And by that time, he had started salivating.

As soon as he was the next person on the line to receive the sweet, Kabir stood there speechless. Speechless and taken aback by the presence of the beautiful woman who was standing in front of him and serving the sweet.

The same thick eyebrows that he had seen a thousand times that arched well on the forehead, eyes as deep as the ocean and at the same time as dreamy as the night star-laden sky, a smile as innocent as a child's giggle, and a few strands of hair that were out of place framing her face well enough.

She smiled at him, and he smiled back, the other men from the queue were restless as they pushed him aside, and the queue kept moving.

Kabir had seen Bhavi. It was her.

How did she know? How had she come here?

Kabir who was now standing away from the line, came forward to speak with her. Bhavi signalled with her eyes strictly not to do so.

Kabir thus went away from her without anyone noticing and sat at a distance watching her distributing the sweets to the men. He pinched himself to check whether this was a dream. But no, it wasn't. The pinch was painful.

She was strikingly beautiful that day, like a single full bloomed rose in an otherwise dried garden, and not a thing had changed since the day Kabir met her in the market for the first time, selling flowers. It was the same Bhavi, and Kabir could not take his eyes off her just like the other day.

It was the best thing that his eyes had seen in a month and the only thing that was on his mind the rest of the day.

The women who had come had prepared one of best meals the men had ever eaten in their life. Roti was served with mutton curry. There was rice with dal, some cucumber raita, and dessert.

As the sun went down that evening, Kabir managed to confront Bhavi at the back of his tent.

Bhavi explained in detail about the trail of events that led her there in the first place.

'You told me you will be back in a week, but almost two weeks passed, and you still didn't come home,' whispered Bhavi.

'You didn't get my letter?' asked Kabir.

'What letter?' I never got any letter. I became so scared and started imagining all the worst possibilities. My fear grew as the days passed by. So, one day, I went to Nisma and asked her about your whereabouts. I pleaded to her, and she eventually revealed that you were somewhere near the borders of Kashmir. I asked her if there was any way of me reaching that place. Initially, she tried to stop me, but after realising how stubborn I was with the fact that I wanted to see you, she secretly revealed to me that the Boss who hired you was looking for some cooks who were ready to relocate to the site. I instantly agreed with her, but she told me a few conditions and it was just one day's work. The conditions were: One, Once I came here, I couldn't go back unless the work got over, and two, I couldn't be related to anybody who was already on the site. She told me not to reveal my true identity to anybody here. As long as I was able to meet you, I was more than happy to abide by all the conditions. Why should I worry when I'm only coming to the place where you are? My only worry was about the kids, but Nisma told me that I can take kids along with me to the site who are under four years with me to the site. If I can take care of them, then, it won't be a problem, she said. She also told me that she could not assure me about the conditions here, and that I had to be prepared for rough conditions. I was ready for everything, but I must tell you that the journey was not easy. There were many such women like me, and we were transported in a truck from Lahore. But the moment I saw you here, all of my pain and fear just flew away. How are you doing by the way, Kabir, I mean, how are you? Is everything okay?'

'I'm fine, Bhavi, but what have you done? And where have you come? Why would you do something insane like this? I had sent you a letter and I think you had departed from Lahore even before my letter could reach you,' said Kabir, holding her cheeks with his hands and taking back her contagious smile. He knew the situation was intense, but he couldn't help but be glad that at least she was here. 'And also, did you just say that you are here for only one day? Means are you leaving tomorrow?'

'I have come for you. I have just come for you, Kabir. But what is this place? It doesn't seem like a marketplace or something. What are you guys practising for all day?'

'Bhavi, answer my question first. Are you all leaving tomorrow?'

'And yes, we are leaving tomorrow. They hired us only for a single day.'

'Oh god. What am I going to do?'

'What happened? And what's been happening here, Kabir? Are

you going to tell me or not?'

'It is a long story, Bhavi, and I will explain that to you later. If I had known earlier that you are going to be coming here in search of me, I would have stopped you, for you have come to a dangerous place. But now that you have come, do not worry about anything else. Whatever it is, we are in this together, and that is all that matters. I will take care of everything. I can't put into words how happy I am to see you, not even in my wildest dreams I would have thought that you would be here with me at this moment. I love you, Jaan.'

Bhavi just smiled back contently.

'Where are the kids? Haven't seen them here.'

'They are fine Kabir. They are sleeping now in the tent.'

'I have to see them once before you leave tomorrow.'

'Okay sure, I will make sure that happens. Leaving that aside, what is it that is bothering you, Kabir? Why are you sounding so panicked and restless?'

Kabir began, holding her hands and bringing them in front of his chest. He said, 'Listen to me, Bhavi. Whatever I'm going to ask you to do tomorrow, I want you to trust me.'

'Of course,' Bhavi nodded.

Kabir continued, 'Just do as exactly as I'm saying. When it is time to leave tomorrow, pack food as much as possible for you and Abhi. The truck that brought you here will come to pick you up as well. I want you to board as the last member on the truck with the kids. As soon as you cross the gate of this campsite, within five hundred metres, on your right you would see a waterfall at a distance. I want you to get down from the truck right away somehow. I don't know what you are going to do to stop the truck. But just get down and keep walking towards the waterfall till you reach it. A few metres away from where the waterfall is hitting the ground, you would see an abandoned temple mandap structure with an intact roof. I want you to be inside it and wait for Vimal.'

'Vimal? Why is he coming there?'

'Bhavi, just listen to me. He will take you and the kids to his place at Srinagar. We are finally going to India, my love.'

'And you, then? When will you be joining us?'

'Bhavi, I want you to leave with the kids first. I will come and meet you guys in Srinagar the next day, I promise.'

Bhavi just stood there looking at Kabir and not knowing what to say.

'Bhavi, please, I want you to trust me. I will come for sure and meet you guys in a day or two. But you have to leave first. Even right now, we are so close to India, just a few kilometres away from the border. We can't leave another opportunity like this. Remember the time at Kartarpur? We were so close, yet we couldn't cross. But we are never leaving our chance this time.'

But… Kabir…'

'Look, I cannot speak to you much longer. Please remember what I have said, and I will meet you tomorrow before you leave. Don't worry about me. I have a job to finish here, and I will return home after that once and for all.'

'What if Vimal doesn't come tomorrow?'

After a long pause, Kabir replied, 'He will. Now, you go to your place. I think my tent mates are coming.'

Chapter Nineteen

D-DAY

October 21, 1947

8 a.m.

The morning breakfast was ready, and the women who were brought in the previous day, were getting ready for their departure from the site. A truck was waiting for them in one corner of the ground. And one by one with their packed baggage, they boarded the truck.

Kabir came with a Quran in his hand and was standing beside the truck. As he had instructed, Bhavi had not boarded the truck until then. Kabir went in search of her at their place but failed to find her. So, he waited for her near the truck, his anxiety increasing with each passing second.

Men were busy having their breakfast in the food counter area, and nobody noticed Kabir so much. Finally, Farooq had also come to start the truck. As soon as he was getting ready to move the truck, there came Bhavi with little Indya in her hands, and was holding Abhi in the other hand. Abhi took little steps toward the truck and

Bhavi slowed down her pace to match his.

When they were near, Kabir masked his face with a shawl, so that, Abhi wouldn't identify and come running to him. Bhavi noticed him waiting near the truck and came near him on her way. Kabir ran his fingers over Indya's scalp and patted Abhi on his shoulders. He then handed out the Quran to Bhavi and gave her something wrapped up in a cloth. He went a little closer to her and whispered, 'Give the Quran to Vimal, and use the cloth bundle when necessary.' He slowly left the place as a few trainers came near the truck to check whether everyone had boarded.

Bhavi hid the Quran and the cloth bundle inside her bag and made her way to the truck. As the truck took a 180-degree turn, it began moving towards the main gate. Kabir gazed at Bhavi, and his eyelids slowly came together and opened, communicating non-verbally that everything would be okay. Bhavi nodded and smiled back at Kabir as a reassuring signal from her end.

As the truck crossed the gates, Bhavi quickly looked at what was inside the cloth bundle. As she opened the knots, to her surprise, she found a gun and remembered Kabir's words, 'Use it when necessary.' She looked outside to her right to find if there was any waterfall. And, within a few minutes, she found one at a distance. So, that was the landmark which Kabir had earlier mentioned.

She quickly pulled out the gun and pointed it at the woman sitting over. They began screaming at the top of their voice, not knowing what to do. They were shocked and scared for their life. She instructed them to make way for her and banged hard from the inside of the truck. Nevertheless, Farooq heard nothing.

The women continued screaming, seeing her point a gun at them. Still, there was no response from Farooq. Bhavi warned the women inside the truck not to tell anyone what she was going to do and with no other option left, she peeked a little outside to find that the road ahead was uneven with pits and cracks.

As the driver slowed down the truck, Bhavi got hold of Abhi, lifted him, and bent down to leave him on the road from a moving truck. He began crying and denied placing his foot on the road. Bhavi managed to leave him down despite his resistance. He started crying hard being left all alone on the roads. Within the next few seconds, as the truck slowed down for the second time, Bhavi jumped out of the truck with Indya in one hand and her bag in the other. She fell with a thud without any proper support to hold on to but managed to safeguard Indya and didn't hurt her.

She ran to console Abhi who was crying on the streets, and as soon as the truck was about to take a turn, she took the kids and disappeared into the forests, and escaped from the eyes of Farooq just at the right moment.

It was a cloudy morning and the sun had just come up. The October winds were blowing hard, and it was as if a heavy downpour was at the store for everyone. She made her way through the pine trees towards the waterfall. She could see her flowing clearly at a distance from the place she was on but was sure that it might take a while to reach the spot as it was quite distant from her.

She kept her feet on the fallen leaves and made her way amidst the shrubs and bushes. She was careful to not step on any tiny creatures that were crawling on the ground.

Finally, she reached the spot and inhaled the damp earthly scent realised why Kabir had spoken so much about this place. It was magnificent. A treasure trove right in the middle of nowhere. The waterfall was pounding over the rocks and had a beautiful serenity pool at its bottom.

She scanned the whole vista of the mandap and found it a few hundred metres away.

She managed to climb inside the mandap and decided to wait for Vimal. Time passed by, and as she was not fully aware of the situation that Kabir was in, she had nothing to worry about for the moment, except the thought that came up now and then, stating, "What if Vimal never came?' 'How long should I wait for him? How am I supposed to reach Lahore with the kids?'

Noon came, and it was still cloudy. Bhavi looked up at the sky. It was perfect but was changing. Huge dark clouds were beginning to take form, standing in the way of sunlight even more.

Bhavi and Abhi had a few bites from the food that she had packed from the campsite earlier that morning. Both of them were bored of staying up there for hours together, doing nothing. Abhi wanted to play in the waters ever since he arrived and began to throw tantrums for the same. With no other option left to pacify him, Bhavi finally gave in and decided to take Abhi to the waters.

She put Indya to sleep and placed her right at the centre of the mandap, carefully wrapped up in a soft woollen towel. She was the most adorable baby Bhavi had ever seen. While she slept, Bhavi ran her fingers gently across her little face and felt the softness of her skin. It still felt surreal to believe that she was the one who had brought this little angel out to the world.

And then, there was Abhi, who was drawn naturally to the pool of waters, the sheer volume and its intensity hardly scaring him. Bhavi was quite surprised by his fondness for the water body. Both of them stayed at a place where the river slowed a bit, and Abhi began sliding into the waters from a sloping edge of a rock at the banks, immersing himself in the river once in a while.

Bhavi stayed with him and made sure he was safe there, at the same time keeping an eye on the baby who was sleeping a few metres away, unaware of the events that were going to unfold.

She stared at the flowing waters, rhythmically gushing one after another and hopping over the rocks, gently turning around the corners over a pebbled riverbed, a few butterflies fluttering over the stream, a picture that looked so calm, yet somehow felt chaotic to Bhavi.

She remembered the last time when they were stranded near a stream. It was in Shabazpur, and how she had to leave the place without Kabir all alone and here she was stranded and left without him this time, too.

She thought about all the possible explanations for Kabir being held up here. But no such assumption made sense to her. She still believed that Kabir was helping Boss with his business. 'But why wasn't he at Srinagar, and what was he doing at this place in the middle of nowhere with hundreds of other men?' All these questions lingered at the back of her mind.

Even in their wildest dreams, who would have thought that those men were planning to wage a war against Kashmir by training the locals?

The sun was about to go down, and so were her hopes. Darkness was descending around her, and Vimal still hadn't reached the place. There was nothing to hold her hopes high other than Kabir's last words, 'Vimal will definitely make it.'

She badly wished they would come true while she waited there for what seemed the longest evening of her life.

As it was getting darker, she decided to go to the mandap and called Abhi, telling him that it was time. She stood up and dusted her dupatta and when she looked back to check on Indya, there was someone else standing there holding the baby. It was a tall guy with round spectacles.

Bhavi got hold of Abhi immediately and made her way to the mandap, and as she got closer, she knew it was none other than Vimal Adityan himself.

There he was.

So, after all these years, he had truly come as Kabir had said.

Vimal took Indya in his arms, and the minute he stared at her gorgeous brown eyes, he knew she was Kabir's daughter.

On their way back home in the car, when Vimal enquired about Kabir, Bhavi showed him the campsite that Kabir was on. Vimal decided to reach the camp and look out for him, but when he reached there, to Bhavi's surprise, the camp was empty. There was no one.

Vimal thoroughly searched the area, and he sensed that something was not right. 'What was Kabir doing here in the India-Pakistan border for all this time? Why did he want me to come now after all these years?' He had no answers to these questions.

By this time, Abhi, who was exhausted from playing the whole evening, conveniently slept on Bhavi's lap in the back seat. She slowly patted him as he drifted to deep slumber.

When Vimal enquired Bhavi whether Kabir had told her anything about the things that were happening around them, Bhavi had no clue about Kabir as he had not revealed anything to her. But she told Vimal what all she had been seeing at the site yesterday.

Hundreds of men stayed in the tents, the security guards at the gate, the one man in an unknown uniform whom they addressed as 'the Officer', and about how she, along with the other women, was hired to cook for them.

Vimal, upon hearing all this, very well knew that Kabir wouldn't call him here for no small reason. He was sure that Kabir would want him to know the real situation he had been in. So, he asked her once again, 'Was there anything at all that Kabir wanted me to know?'

Bhavi opened her bag and saw the pistol and also noticed the Quran. That's when she remembered Kabir's words to give the Quran to Vimal.

'When I was about to leave the place, he gave me the Quran and asked me to give it to you,' she said as she took it out and handed him the Quran.

Vimal stopped the car, opened it, and skimmed through its pages.

When he had reached the last few pages, he noticed that there was something written on it.

His heart momentarily skipped a beat as he was reading the write-up. When he almost finished, he realised the danger that the state of Kashmir was in, and also wondered why Kabir still hadn't escaped from the rebel group. *He is risking his own life for his country,* he thought.

In the writings, Kabir had mentioned what all had happened to him, how he was hired, what happened at the campsite, the plan that the Officer had narrated to them, and everything else.

He ended up with the line, '*I have lost two of my greatest friends, and all I have now is only you, Vimal. Please do something and put an end to this war before things go out of hand and take care of Bhavi and the kids until I come back.*' It was signed "Kabir Khan".

Vimal knew that he was short on time. So, he quickly gathered up his spirits. He was very particular that his dear friend's efforts should never go in vain. He started the car and drove straight towards his home in Srinagar.

Seeing the mere look on Vimal's face after reading the Quran, Bhavi knew something was wrong. But when asked, Vimal chose to remain noncommittal.

The journey to Srinagar was not easy as thunderstorms began rumbling with intense lightning now and then, followed by a heavy downpour. Bhavi could hardly see the outside.

The rainfall was torrential and was hammering the roof of the vehicle. Bhavi looked outside the window and the sky was tar black. The roads were filled with puddles as the rain became heavier.

Bhavi asked Vimal whether they could halt somewhere nearby to take shelter, and then, continue the journey once the rainfall intensity has decreased, to which Vimal replied that 'We have to get to the home as early as possible.'

The journey was scary for the new-born baby as she wouldn't stop crying the whole time. No amount of pacification could calm her down as thunderstorms kept roaring furiously at the backdrop.

Finally, they all reached home after hours of strenuous journey.

As soon as they reached home, Vimal introduced them to his mother, Sundari, who, the minute she saw Bhavi and the kids, took them under her wings.

Vimal enquired his mother about his father's whereabouts and came to know that he was at the court with Raja. He placed Bhavi's belongings in the guest room and immediately left to meet his dad. Both Bhavi and his mom were clueless about why he was in such a hurry that he left within a few minutes of arriving home.

Chapter Twenty

CHRYSANTHEMUMS

October 21, 6 p.m.

Ind-Pak Border

Meanwhile, at the campsite, men were arranged into separate troops, and by the evening, everyone had vacated the training camp. Tents were pulled out, and all the arms and ammunition were packed and transported to a different site very close to the border. Men were given one last motivational speech by the Boss before they departed.

They were joined by the rest of the nine thousand men from the Srinagar-front group who were trained separately in separate camps. All of them were now stationed together just two miles away from the India-Pakistan border, ready to launch the attack.

The next day was their D-Day. The day they had waited for days had come.

The star troop were the frontline attackers, who were trained with all the advanced armoury and had this huge task of carrying the success of the entire war on their shoulders.

Kabir and his team were instructed to carry and move the boxes of ammunition and help the other men in transporting food and other essential materials that were needed for camping. They were taking up the job of load men, exactly what Kabir was hired for, weeks ago.

Thunderstorms were striking the sky now and then. There was Kabir, not having a clue about what he was going to do. There was no way back now that the rebellion had finally begun. And so, he decided not to quit in the middle, because though he couldn't stop the rebellion from happening, he was determined to cause enough trouble to this militia and slow their pace somehow.

He was a one-man army representing India inside the militia itself, which could prove to be deadly for the group if Kabir was successful in his attempts. He wanted to delay the group somehow in reaching Srinagar.

The rest was in Vimal's hands in passing down the information to the Indian army. Kabir had to delay as much as possible and give the precious time that was needed for the Indian troops to mobilise to Jammu and Kashmir.

Every single man from the Srinagar-front assembled at the site. There were around ten thousand of them altogether. They were all geared up and ready for their mission. Finally, the time had come for one of the most important rebellions in the history of India that would forever change the course of the lives of people living in the state of Jammu and Kashmir.

It was the beginning of a never-ending war.

Who would have even thought a small unorganised rebellion would turn into something massive of this size?

Thunderstorms booming and striking the world outside sounded exactly like the turmoil that Kabir felt inside. Events were happening so fast and at a rapid pace that Kabir himself couldn't plan his next move.

On the morning of October 22, as they had already planned, rebels who were the residents of Kashmir began their attacks in small pockets throughout the state, thus dispersing the J&K forces from the main outposts and roadways. They were successful in their first move.

October 22

J&K capital: Srinagar

It had been a few hours since Vimal had left the house. Bhavi had changed into a fresh set of clothes. She had some hot soup, and while wondering what Vimal was hiding, she went into the guest room and saw the Quran that Kabir had given placed on the table.

She opened the pages and was shocked to death by reading all that he had mentioned. How ignorant had she been all this time without knowing the problem that Kabir was into? She choked for words and ran downstairs to find Vimal's mom. She cried to her whether there was any way to contact Vimal.

October 22, 6 p.m.

Muzaffarabad

It was evening by then, and the group began their invasion into the town of Muzaffarabad. They marched on foot in the front, followed by the trucks behind. They divided themselves into two groups. While the first group comprised around 6000 men, who went forward, the second group remained as a backup in case of any emergency. Kabir was allocated to the latter group.

The first encounter with the militia was at the Muzaffarabad outpost at the outskirts of town. Since most of the J&K forces were spread inside the state to tackle the local rebel problem, the men at the outpost were heavily outnumbered. They never saw it coming.

The star-troop opened fire at the few soldiers who were stationed there and caught hold of the outpost even before they could pass on the information by cutting all their communication lines to the state.

That was followed by the killing, loot, arson, rape, and kidnapping of non-Muslim women that took place at Muzaffarabad and were encouraged by their Officer in charge.

It was estimated that around 5000 Hindus and Sikhs were massacred, and more than 1000 women were kidnapped during those two days at Muzaffarabad.

The militia rejoiced in their first taste of victory and continued to march forward towards Uri. When this information reached the backup team, they celebrated in elation, too, and Kabir had to use all his willpower to remain silent.

October 22, 11 p.m.

Muzaffarabad Outpost

As the second group with 4000 men were then stationed at the Muzaffarabad outpost, they camped there for the night and tents were laid. Kabir and his men were instructed to bring the dry wooden logs from the truck and start a fire.

He got an idea and made his way to the truck before anyone and quickly cut the tarpaulin that was covering the truck with a hand knife that he had been hiding under his kurta, which led to the collapse of the tarpaulin and poured down all the rainwater that had been stagnated at the top of it. It moistened all the wooden logs and when they tried to light a fire using these wet logs, they failed terribly.

After trying for many hours, the men finally gave up and shivered all night in the freezing coldness, deprived of fire to warm themselves and hot water to drink.

The next morning, the group that had suffered enough last night woke up tired. More than a hundred men had developed frostbite in their extremities as it had rained all day, and the night was extremely cold and wet. The rest were severely tired without the proper rest.

The news that the front-line troop was successfully marching towards Uri, ruthlessly killing everyone on their way, boosted the spirit of the backup team.

October 23

By then, Vimal had informed all that Kabir had revealed to him to his father and to the other Ministers at Raja Hari Singh's court. He realised the intensity of the issue and brought this information to the ears of the Maharaja and the Chief of Security Forces of Jammu and Kashmir.

Initially, they were reluctant to believe that this story would even be true. But then, after seeing the scattered internal rebellions throughout the state on the previous day just like Vimal had said, they were left with no other option other than to believe him.

Raja was still a little hesitant because he was so adamant in believing that nothing could cause harm to him or his rule. But the Chief took the matters seriously as they were not able to establish communication from the Muzaffarabad outpost until then.

Matters escalated and the J&K forces were organised and scattered throughout the major points of the state. Guards were increased in Jammu and Gilgit. But maximum forces stayed back at Srinagar to defend the capital in case of any attack.

In the meantime, the front-line attackers of the rebels were making their way towards Uri.

October 24

URI

By now, the news of the invasion had already reached the ears of the state, and Brigadier Rajinder Singh and his 200 men were sent from the capital Srinagar towards Uri to safeguard and stop it from falling into the hands of the enemy.

Brigadier Rajinder Singh and his troops met with the front-line rebels head-on at the outskirts of Uri, and both the team suffered casualties. The Officer dressed up as one of them was the one leading the front-line army of the rebels. He immediately called a thousand men from the backup team of the rebels to assist them.

Kabir and his men were then mobilised to the site in trucks.

When the backup team had arrived, Brigadier Rajinder Singh and his men, who had already suffered enough casualties, were heavily outnumbered and with no other option at hand, they decided to retreat to the capital.

On their way, they crossed an important bridge which was the only motorable road to the capital and decided to hold their position at the headend. When the rebel troops tried to advance with their truck, the Brigadier's team was running short of ammunition and struggled to hold the enemy forces at the tail end of the bridge.

At this point, when everyone was busy with the firing, Kabir slowly snuck away from the crowd and went behind the trucks. He quickly took out his hand knife and bent down when no one was noticing and pierced his knife hard into the tyres of the truck strong enough to puncture a front wheel and a rear wheel.

He repeated this for five other trucks which were carrying heavy boxes of arms and ammunition along with other camping essentials.

By evening, as the rebels were resolute in advancing their trucks into the bridge, despite Brigadier's team giving their best in holding them, they finally decided to bomb and blasted the bridge, leaving the rebel troops stranded at the tail end.

With the destruction of the only motorable bridge that they had to cross in order to reach the capital, the rebels were left stuck at the other end.

That night, they decided to camp at Uri right outside the broken bridge. A small team of fifty members split themselves from the rest of the group and went in search of other pathways to cross the river and enter Uri.

October 25

URI

At dawn, the men returned to the camp with a piece of good news after having successfully found another route traversing the river at its shortest and shallowest point.

They regrouped themselves and rerouted to the other way, and that was when they noticed that six of their trucks had been punctured. The Officer concluded that someone from the J&K forces would have snuck inside their camp the previous night and done this.

As a result, the Officer instructed the men from the backup team to carry the heavy boxes from those six trucks manually from that point. The boxes weighed hundreds of kilos and carrying them for miles seemed like an impossible task, but no one dared to question Officer's orders.

The group began their journey on foot to cross the river. The Brigadier and his men, though they were only 200 against this army of thousands, fought till their last breath and in the process, Brigadier Rajinder Singh lost his life.

After losing their leader, the few men who were remaining retreated to the next big station on the way to the capital, which is Baremullah.

Brigadier Rajinder Singh, known as the Saviour of Kashmir, was an officer in the Jammu and Kashmir state forces. He briefly served as the Chief of Staff of State Forces and died at Uri while successfully hampering the advancement of the Pakistan tribal raiders for two days, during which Maharaja Hari Singh acceded Kashmir to India and the Indian troops were airlifted to Kashmir for its defence. He was posthumously awarded Maha Vir Chakra, India's second highest military decoration.

The rebels' original plan was to be in Baremullah by October 25. But they were lagging due to two reasons: One, Brigadier and his men who blew the bridge had rendered them impossible to cross the bridge; and two, as the trucks were punctured, a journey that usually took a few hours now took an entire day as men were carrying all the materials manually and walking. This slowed the pace of the entire group drastically.

Meanwhile, this caused a delay for two more days at Uri, which gave the J&K officials enough time to strike a deal with India and get help from the Indian army. Maharaja, along with Vimal and his dad, flew to Delhi and asked help from Sardar Vallabhai Patel to send in Indian troops inside Kashmir to strengthen their defence.

October 26

The raiders reached the power station at Mahura, and as per their plan, they destroyed the power station that supplied electricity to Srinagar. As a result, the capital city faced a complete blackout.

When this information was passed on to the J&K officials in Delhi, they realised they were running out of time and if the decisions were to be postponed even further, then it would be late, and their capital would be down any minute.

Vimal even revealed to the officials that they were 30,000 men strong and had already planned an attack on three fronts, and this was just the Srinagar-front rebels.

As the fear of losing his state to the raiders gripped Maharaja Hari Singh, he thus signed the Instrument of Accession and Kashmir joined India on the evening of October 26th.

Maharaja even appointed Sheikh Abdulla as the Emergency Administrator of Jammu and Kashmir, fled Srinagar, and left for safety to Jammu. India accepted the Instrument of Accession, and soon after, Indian troops were airlifted to Srinagar.

By then, the raiders had almost reached Baremullah, and Kabir knew that they were only thirty miles away from Srinagar. The Indian troops still hadn't reached Baremullah to stop the rebels. He knew he had to do something big in order to change the course of events that were to take place.

While they were camping at the outskirts of Baremullah, Kabir mustered all his courage and went near a truck that was loaded with grenades and ammo. Then, he did exactly as he had been taught during their grenade class, pulled the trigger, and threw it inside the truck to detonate. He had a few seconds before it blasted, so he ran for his life and took cover immediately.

The truck exploded and sent shock waves for hundreds of metres. It blew up another truck nearby. Metal shreds splattered in all directions.

Men ran to take cover, and a few who were nearby were injured, along with the Officer himself, who was bleeding profusely from a metal shred that had torn his thighs and injured his arteries.

The team watched helplessly as the trucks kept burning continuously along with all its contents.

As the Officer lost a lot of blood, his consciousness wavered and was taken to the medical team. Kabir, who was not selected for the star-troop, was trained in first aid, and after the medical team had immobilised his leg, he was started on fluids to combat his blood loss.

Kabir stayed back with the Officer, and when everyone left the tent for a brief moment, he quickly loaded the syringe with morphine and injected it into the Officer's IV line. The dose was sufficient enough to keep him in an unconscious state for more than 24 hours.

And since he remained non-responsive for many hours, the next in power to him was a Junior Commissioner Officer, who ordered fifteen men to safely transport him back to Pakistan and give him the proper medical attention.

Men who were given the daunting task of carrying the heavy armoury boxes on shoulders and the ones who had developed frostbite on day one were physically exhausted and weak.

Adding to it, more than half of the men were heavily starving and with their leader taken down, slowly, the morale of the troop decreased steadily. All the *josh* and the wish to avenge Kashmir were hanging on the thread.

All of this delayed the group's advancement into Baremullah, and the small mishaps that were caused inside their group by Kabir proved lethal as it provided the most valuable time for Vimal to pass on the information to the Maharaja, and thereby, got help from the Indian army.

October 27, 4 a.m.

Baremullah

The raiders under the new leadership of a Junior Commissioner Officer reached Baremullah, and instead of swiftly advancing towards the capital which was only a few miles away, the rebels

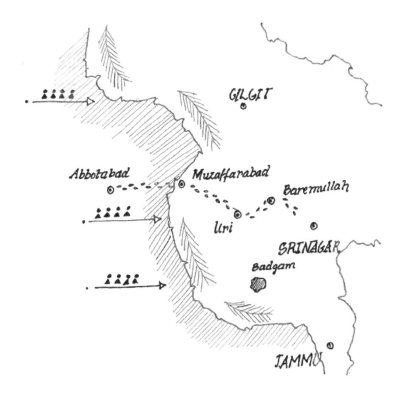

without their Captain made the biggest tactical mistake staying at Baremullah, and chose to loot and pillage, plundering the prosperous town of Baremullah. And by doing so, they lost their most valuable time.

They rounded the town from all directions and came shooting their way down the hills. They climbed over the hospital walls and began firing at the patients inside the wards.

A 20-year-old nurse who tried to protect a Hindu woman who had just given birth to her baby was shot first, and then, the mother was killed next. Both of them collapsed on the hospital floor instantly.

'With very little protection, the prosperous town of Baremullah bore the brunt of the raiders' greed and lust as the tribals halted their advance ransacking the town over the next few days.'—Air Vice Marshal Arjun Subramaniam.

The attack devastated the Baremullah people. The homes of Hindus and Muslims were looted, shops were plundered; even places of worship were not spared. And they tore down mandirs and desecrated masjids, followed by a mayhem of killings and rapes.

Hundreds of Hindu, Sikh, and Muslim women were raped and abducted, and many were carried away to Rawalpindi, Peshawar, Lahore, and to many other towns of Pakistan.

On just that day alone, the intruders had massacred more than ten thousand Baremullah residents. This delay at the Baremullah decided the fate of the Kashmir invasion.

Sheikh Abdullah, the most popular leader of Jammu and Kashmir, who later went on to become the first Prime Minister of J&K after its accession to India, described the tribal invasion at the UN Security Council. 'The raiders came to our land, massacred thousands of people—mostly Hindus and Sikhs but Muslims, too—and abducted thousands of girls, Hindus, Sikhs, and Muslims alike, looted our property and almost reached the gates of our summer capital, Srinagar.'

Indian Army Enters The Battle

By the morning of October 27, the first battalion of the Sikh regiment under the leadership of commanding officer Lieutenant Colonel Dewan Ranjit Rai of the Indian army had reached the Badgam airfields of Jammu and Kashmir from Delhi.

Before they landed, they were not even sure whether the airfields were in friendly control or not. They circled around the airfields for quite some time, until finally, they were sure that the fields were in friendly control and landed. From there, the troops proceeded to Srinagar.

The raiders, choosing to stay and plunder Baremullah, instead of swiftly moving forward and entering Srinagar, gave Lieutenant Colonel Rai sufficient time to reach Srinagar and plan their positions in and around the capital city.

By 7 p.m., the Indian army had strengthened their defensive positions at Srinagar and Colonel Rai with the best of his men decided to move forward towards Baremullah to meet the enemy head on.

The Indian troops, though small at that time when compared to the invading raiders, were thumped up and mentally strong as they had carefully planned each and every move ahead.

They made their way towards Baremullah from Srinagar at midnight, and the rebels had no clue that the Indian army were on their way to the scene.

Kabir, broken by all that he had seen in the past few days, was totally exhausted and had slowly lost the life inside him. He was just a lump of flesh and bones; sick and lifeless.

The past five days had been mentally demanding for him, and he had come this far only with one single hope that his letter would have reached Vimal and he would have come for him, and then, Bhavi would have passed on the Quran to him. But as days went by, his hope gradually reduced with every passing hour, and adding to all these, it had been many days since he had had a proper meal.

He was thirsty, he was hungry, he was worn out, homesick, and what not. Every single thing happening around him was bothering him.

He thought about the last day he met Bhavi at the camp. Maybe, he thought, he should have shared everything and cried to her, letting out all the pain that he had locked inside his heart and everything that was bothering him. He thought that would have made him feel a little bit lighter. But he just couldn't reveal the dangerous situation that he was facing as she would have never left the camp without him.

He sat on the stairs of a damaged building of a school at the main street of Baremullah and witnessed the chaos in front of him.

The vista in front of him was covered in a haze of smoke at the backdrop of the crying of women and wailing of small children. He looked at a man who was lying lifeless in front him. It would have been hours since his death. The look on his face haunted Kabir.

He had done everything in his capacity to stop this war from progressing, yet here he was—still witnessing it at every single point with his own eyes.

Suddenly, he quivered on hearing the raiders screaming at the top of their voice pointing the east. Kabir stood up and took a moment to realise that it was the Indian army. They had come, thank the Lord. They had finally come.

The smile on his face, the moment he saw them, was all encompassing. One could easily say that he was merrier than the day he saw his daughter for the first time.

The rebels panicked on seeing the Indian army and began ruthlessly firing on them, giving their level best to repel them and proceed towards Srinagar. It took some time for them to realise the mistake that they had done by halting at Baremullah. The Indian troops counter attacked and went on a complete attacking mode.

The raiders gave an equally tough fight. Though the Indian army were outnumbered, they were successful in stopping them from advancing. As the Indian army came further inside their territory, the rebels planned another tactical move and diverted some men from their team to the Badgam airfields with the mission of capturing the airfields, thereby cutting the reinforcements for the army from Delhi.

The Indian army quickly noted this move of theirs and sent their best 50 soldiers back to the Badgam airfields to safeguard it under the command of Major Somnath Sharma. Access to the airfield was very crucial from the Indian army's standpoint because that was the only way reinforcements could arrive at Srinagar border, both quickly and continuously throughout the war. They were given the command, 'Enter into Srinagar airfield. Hold the airfield at any cost, until reinforcements arrive.'

Major Sharma and his men were outnumbered 1:7 against the enemy and suffered heavy casualties. Despite heavy losses, Major and his team repelled the enemy attack on the airfield and saved it from being captured by the raiders. This resulted in the airfield remaining in the control of Indian armed forces for the remainder of the war. Major Sharma played a crucial role in achieving his mission but lost his life during the battle. His last message to his unit was, 'The enemies are only 50 yards from us. We are heavily outnumbered. We are under devastating fire. I shall not withdraw an inch but will fight to the last man and the last round.' For his bravery and sacrifice in the battle, he was posthumously awarded Param Vir Chakra, India's highest military honour.

Lieutenant Colonel Dewan Ranjit Rai lost his life in a machine gun crossfire while fighting the invaders at Baremullah. October 27 is celebrated as the Infantry Day by the Indian army. He played a key role in saving Kashmiri valley from the invaders and was posthumously awarded the Maha Vir Chakra and was the first recipient of MVC in the independent India.

Kabir's role was over. He knew the time had come for him to flee this arena. Not knowing which would be a safer haven for him to hide, he ran and ran, passing through a few narrow streets and went as far from the battle firings as possible.

He ran in the opposite direction of Baremullah, and after some time, at the outskirts of the town, he stumbled upon an open field filled with fully blossomed yellow chrysanthemums. He stopped there and bent down to catch his breath and as he woke up, he witnessed one of the most beautiful sunrises that he had ever seen.

The sun slowly came peeking at a distance with the horizon tinged red and cast a pinkish hue across the morning sky. He took a minute to appreciate the light of dawn falling over the orange blanket of fully bloomed chrysanthemums that were spread for acres at the backdrop of the chorus melody of the birds drifting in.

He saw thousands of chrysanthemums right in front of his eyes glowing vibrantly in the morning light. It was a sight to behold, and the sunlight just lit the scene. He wished he had his Kodak camera with him to freeze the moment. He continued his way trotting through the middle of the chrysanthemum field as a gentle breeze hit him with a familiar scent and stopped in the middle, suddenly, as he heard noises and found movements on the other end. Little did he know that the Indian army would surround Baremullah from all sides.

He imagined it would be the Indian army as he could see military uniforms making way from the bushes hundreds of metres apart. He quickly raised both his arms to notify them that he was friendly.

He was indeed a friendly, perhaps the only and the most important friendly from the entire enemy army, wearing a vest with the number 149 who was responsible for the Indian army arriving to the scene in the first place.

It took a few seconds for him to realise that he was still wearing the vest, and that his kurta was soiled, and both his face and hands had grease stain all over it. And before he could even think, at the wink of a second, a 0.303 calibre bullet went right through his chest, tearing his ribs apart.

His entire world stopped for a brief moment, and as soon as he regained, the next bullet went right through his skull; this time, Kabir didn't even hear the bullet coming to him.

The bullet caused a gaping hole right at the centre of his forehead, splashing his brain out as blood came gushing out from the wound. He fell to the ground as a pool of blood formed around him and the musty scent of the chrysanthemums finally made their way through his nose.

Two years ago

On June 10, 1945, Kabir and Bhavi got married at her home at Rawalpindi.

It was a beautiful day. It had been raining then for the past few days, but on that day, the sun finally came out breaking the clouds.

A small mandap was set up inside Bhavi's house in Rawalpindi with only close relatives from either side of the family as guests. Their marriage was presided over by Daya's father, Bhattacharya chanting Sanskrit mantras, not a word of which Kabir understood.

The entire ceremony was alien to him. The only Hindu wedding that he had witnessed before that was Daya's and Laxmi's. It had been two years since their marriage, and their son, Abhimanyu, was just a year old.

Abhi was chubby and cranky as a child, and the adults kept switching him as he would not stay put in one person's lap. He would not rest unless he was placed on Kabir's lap. Daya was beside Kabir the whole time, helping him understand the rituals.

While most of the guests were gossiping about this inter-religious wedding, Kabir's father, who was solely responsible for that marriage, was immune to all such comments. He had single-handedly convinced all his relatives and had brought them to the wedding from Punjab.

Religions meant nothing to him. 'Different religions are just different ways of worshipping the one true God,' he would say very often.

Seeing his only son getting married was one of the happiest moments in his life. He smiled at Kabir and there he was, in a creamy white silk kurta, with neatly combed hair and trimmed beard, smiling back at him.

Hours went by, and rituals went one after another. The sun had finally set, and the darkness was setting in. Kabir kept wondering how long these rituals were going to take. He started becoming restless and tired. That's when Laxmi, Raziya and the other ladies accompanied Bhavi to the mandap.

Bhavi was all decked up, looking drop-dead gorgeous, wearing a crimson-red silk lehenga paired with a rust orange dupatta with golden Zari work. The dupatta belonged to her mother. She had carefully treasured it all those years. She wanted a piece of her mom with her on her wedding day.

Her lehenga skirt was hand-sewn with golden thread embroidery and intricate zardozi work. Her entire wedding outfit was a gift from Kabir's family.

Her face was adorned with a golden *nath* (a nose accessory) that went from her nose and behind her ears to the hairline. Her Borla peeped out from the centre of her hairline like a morning sun coming out from the horizon and it slid right and left as she kept moving her head, her wavy hair neatly braided and decorated with *mogra* (jasmine). The white flowers very well complemented her red lehenga, her palms decorated in red with henna that was applied the previous night. Her bangles dangled every time she moved her hands.

The best part was her bright red bindi, affixed just a little above the point where her eyebrows met. With all of those, Bhavi was no less than a goddess that day.

Kabir couldn't take his eyes off her as she went near to sit beside him, blushing. That moment, which they both had been waiting for all these years, finally came true when Kabir applied sindoor on her forehead.

Their eyes met for the first time that day and it was love, just pure love. And that was followed by many secret glances exchanged between each other throughout the day.

Love was filled in the air, and so was the smell of fresh chrysanthemums and their unique musky scent. And for a brief moment, even the elders had completely forgotten their differences to celebrate the union of the young couple.

Daya was already in tears. Kabir's dad was no exception and Ibhu ran out of words to bless the new couple.

They say the sense of smell is closely linked with memory more than any of our other senses. Till date, the smell of fresh chrysanthemums would evoke memories of their wedding day to Kabir.

They took the *Saat Pheras* and went seven circles around the sacred fire together, promising each other a lifetime of happiness and all the goodness in the world. It was a beautiful day, easily one of the best days of Kabir's life.

He remembered that day just like yesterday. He remembered every bit of it even on his last day.

The End.

* * * *

EPILOGUE

And with tears in her eyes and a deep sigh, she lived the story all over again. Indya finished the story that had begun with her. On the last page, she found a black-and-white picture of her father, Vimal, and Daya together, happily smiling with arms wrapped around each other's shoulders with ragged edges of the photograph abruptly cut after Daya.

Ibhu was cut out from the picture by Abhi when Bhavi had told him the real story of what happened back at Sohawa that night.

She stared at the picture and realised what all her dad and mom had gone through to bring her to India, and how foolish she was to even think of leaving India.

No words could describe how Abhi's story made her feel even after all those years, and how proud she was to get Abhimanyu as her brother every time she read any of his work. Some are truly blessed with pen and words, and so was he. He lived a good life, he lived his father's life, as a celebrated writer of the country.

She opened the Quran, which was on the table beside her bed, and quickly turned to the last few pages and glazed her fingers over her father's script. Most of the ink had already faded, and with what was left, she could make out his last words. They were, 'Take care of Bhavi and the kids until I come.'

But he never did come.

No matter how certain death is, when it comes—no one is prepared for it, and it truly takes a heavy toll on the beloved ones.

Kabir lost his life, yet he succeeded in bringing Indya to India. He died for his country in his country.

Indya got carried away by her world of thoughts and came back when Jothi came inside the room with a phone.

It was Kalindi, who was on the line, her granddaughter.

(And what Kalindi grew up to be is for another book.)

What really happened after India entered the battle?

The war that began on October 22, 1947, went on for more than a year, that is, until 5 January 1949. The result of the war was the establishment of the ceasefire line as per the intervention of the United Nations.

Even after the independence of India and Pakistan, each one of their armies was still under the command of the British Officers.

The British officers, initially, refused the entry of the Pakistan soldiers, citing the accession of Kashmir to India. But later, they relented, and the Pakistani armies entered the war shortly afterwards, and the war dragged for months. The Indian army repelled the Pakistani forces slowly away from the centre of the state towards the border.

But the intensity of the conflict and the inability to foresee a quick end to the conflict to expel the Pakistani forces led Indian leaders to approach the United Nations. The UN brokered between the two nations and fronts solidified gradually along, resulting in the establishment of the Ceasefire line, which later came to be known as the Line of Control (LoC).

The inconclusive results of the war still affect the geopolitics of both the countries with Pakistan controlling roughly one-third of Kashmir (Azad Kashmir and Gilgit-Baltistan) and India controlling the rest (Kashmir Valley, Jammu, and Ladakh). The war ended with more than 6000 military casualties from Indian side and over 20000 casualties from Pakistan's side.

AUTHOR'S NOTE

There are many things in life that we take for granted, and freedom tops the list—the freedom that was brought to us with the sacrifice of thousands of lives.

Indian citizens of today did not participate in the freedom struggle, and maybe that's one of the main reasons we don't realise the value of freedom.

What is freedom? I mean, how important is freedom? The depth of the answer to these questions can be found only in a situation where freedom had been denied to us.

Can someone imagine a situation that forces you to disown your native land and home and relocate to a land which is unknown and far away? Can an imaginary political line divide a single piece of land into two different nations with individual notions, and unfortunately, when you happen to remain in the country which followed the notion which is entirely you against your beliefs and practices? What if the piece of land, which was once considered as heaven, has now turned out to be a realm of evils and sufferings?

What would be the exact mindset of the people when they are forced to leave everything, along with those memories, for a place where everything should be started from scratch? Nevertheless, that's exactly what happened to millions of people who were forced to relocate during the India-Pakistan partition. And this relocation due to the partition has cost the lives of nearly 2 million people. Many people went missing, leaving no traces about their whereabouts. Above all, it led to the greatest refugees' crisis the world history has ever witnessed. These incidents raised many questions within me:

What are boundary lines?

What are nationalities?

How significant are they?

Also, who gave the authority to draw those boundary lines in the first place?

In the case of India and Pakistan, Sir Radcliffe was responsible for this boundary line. Imagine if he had drawn the line 5 kilometres inside the existing Pakistan border. The people who are currently labelled as "Pakistanis" would have been called "Indians", and vice-versa. Thinking of such scenarios, made me realise how irrelevant those boundaries and nationalities are. During the COVID-19 outbreak, the boundary lines couldn't stop the virus from spreading, and we fought together for humanity.

So, if boundaries and nationalities are irrelevant, then why should human lives be spared in a fight for land?

In contrast, a cricket match between, say, India and South Africa is just a match. Whereas a cricket match between India and Pakistan is treated like a war. The amount of hatred that we Indians have for Pakistani players and vice versa is still a never-ending war and will not end unless one side is annihilated completely. This is just for a cricket match. Has someone ever realised why we share so much of hatred with our neighbouring State, Pakistan?

Why?

Is it because we fought for the same freedom and got independence on different dates? Or is it because they are non-Hindus?

If they are non-Hindus, then, so are most of the Australians, South Africans, and Sri Lankans.

We are friendly with England, the country who have ruled us and looted us, but not Pakistan who fought for independence along with us side by side. The intention is not to spread hatred, but only to bring more clarity on this issue. Yes, the English have ruled us for hundreds of years. And they have also ruled Canada, Australia, Singapore, South Africa, and many such nations. The British colonising us is a thing from the past, and it's over! And we are done with it, too. If we can get over the British, then why not Pakistan?

Let's leave cricket aside. Have you ever thought of the soldiers who died and are still dying every day in the India-Pakistan borders from 1947 till now?

Giving lives for freedom is fine, giving lives demanding a separate nation is also okay, but why are the soldiers from either side dying till now even after 75 years of partition? Is it only because we are not two friendly nations? Can't we ever have a friendly border with our neighbouring nations? It's funny to realise that we want to be friends with Russia and America, but not with Pakistan.

This war between us doesn't seem to have an end. But this war is totally ridiculous and pointless when we think of the fact that we are literally brothers and sisters from a single mother. Both Pakistanis and Indians have fought for the same freedom from the British. The partition was only a side effect of the freedom movement. We have been the same family since time immemorial. And suddenly, we are enemies for lifetime only because we belonged to two different religions.

Everything that man had created until now had only created divisions. Different countries, different religions, different castes, different sects, and everything has only been creating differences among us. But it's high time that we realise and forget our differences and celebrate each other. Believe me when I say this:

being together is truly a superpower, if not the greatest of all superpowers.

We are much more related to Pakistan and Bangladesh than any other nations.

After 75 years, regrets are now meaningless. We have to accept the fact that we have been divided long before in the name of different religions, but should we still continue to nurture the hatred that we have for each other?

Now that we have discussed on the people who crossed the borders for survival, have you ever thought about the people who decided to stay back?

The current Muslims in India, and the Hindus and the Sikhs of Pakistan decided to stay back in spite of being given separate nations. They stayed back in their respective countries in spite of knowing that they would be much safer in the other country. Still, our Islamic friends chose India. They chose us, only with the hope that we would take good care of them. They believed in us. They believed in the secularism of our nation. They believed they would be treated well, and no harm would arise to them. Doesn't that require sheer guts? And shouldn't we all just celebrate them for choosing India?

The Muslims who stayed back in India after the partition are our greatest gifts. The same for the Hindus and the Sikhs who stayed back in Pakistan. They are Pakistan's gifts. All of them should be treasured.

I'm sure everyone of us would have at least had one friend from Islamic religion. Have you ever asked, why their ancestors chose to stay back in India? And have they ever felt bad for staying back? Were they happy with the decision that their grandparents had taken? If given a chance to move, would they have still chosen to stay in India?

I asked these questions to my friends, and it gave a whole different outlook on the concept of nationalism. I'm very much a patriotic person, but I don't believe in boundary lines. Indians, Pakistanis, Bhutanese, Nepalese—all are one and the same when you erase the boundary lines in between.

I'm ending it here with a heavy heart and with lots of hope.

Thank you.

Would love to hear from you.

Reach me at authorkeerth@gmail.com.

MY TEAM

And, over to my team,

1. My hearty gratitude to Jeya Arthi (currently pursuing Law at SOEL, Taramani) a.k.a my Ilak, for all that you have ever done to me and standing by my side through the thick and thin. You are the greatest gift that Amma and Appa would have ever given to me. I have always considered you as the most intelligent and  beautiful woman I know. Thank you for being my honest critic. Every time I see you, I only see me. I love you and I'm proud of you. Guys, for all of you who didn't know who Ilak is—she is my younger sister and my best friend. From reading early drafts to giving advice on the cover, and deciding the publishers to editing the chapters, she owned it all.

2. Baskar, (final year architecture student from Anna University, Guindy) my junior from school and Ilak's classmate—the man behind all the brilliant illustrations in this book. From spending hours of brainstorming to working your ass-off to bring into life what I had envisioned, and remaining patient the whole

time—you deserve a big thank you, man. I wouldn't have asked for a better illustrator than you. And, I'm really happy that you are in my team.

[Fun fact—All three of us belonged to the same school, Pushpalata Vidya Mandir, Tirunelveli.]

3. And lastly, the man, who boarded the ship at the last minute, yet played the most important role in proofreading my entire manuscript. I should acknowledge the extraordinary debt I owe to you, Dr. Jayanth, Faculty of English Department at Anna University, Chennai. Thank you so  much for sparing your time for me and my story in spite of your hectic schedule and encouraging me for taking this creative attempt. I have no idea what I would have done without you. Thank you, sir.

INKFEATHERS PUBLISHING

India's Most Author Friendly Publishing House

Stay updated about the latest books, anthologies, events, exclusive offers, contests, product giveaways and other things that we do to support authors.

 Inkfeathers Publishing

 @InkfeathersPublishing

 @_Inkfeathers

 @Inkfeathers

 Inkfeathers.com

We'd love to connect with you!

Made in the USA
Coppell, TX
26 August 2022

82101620R00121